OF CURSES AND SCANDALS

JULIE KRAMER

To my family, for standing with me through it all and listening to my crazy ideas

To Lea and KD, for being the best friends a girl could ask for

To Crystal, for being an amazing photographer, and Dalton, for being an amazing fan

And to my readers, for taking a chance on me. I hope you like it!

Blurb

Magic is teenage sorceress Scandal Becker's world, and she even works with the police to help solve cases. When the federal government appoint their own teen sorcerer to bring in a magical arms dealer, Scandal must find some way to work with him. When threats are made against the city that Scandal loves, the identity of the villain is no longer clear and Scandal has a difficult decision to make, which side should she choose; bad or good. If she chooses good, can she do it without the aid of magic?

Of Curses & Scandals is the new novel from author Julie Kramer – if you love young adult fiction and magic, this is the book for you!

Chapter One

There were many, many perks to being a sorceress. I could heat up lukewarm food with a snap of my fingers, sketch out a quick tracking spell to find my favorite scarf—the one that somehow ended up under my bed—and could heal a paper cut with barely a thought. Magic did have its drawbacks, like anything else. Building a tracking spell for anything bigger than a house cat makes me mildly nauseous, and trying to find a person is a sure sign that a long nap is soon to follow. Like, within ten minutes, fifteen at the most. And not just a short nap either, a quick power nap to recharge your batteries. No, this kind of nap could be better compared to a bear in hibernation, where I was so deeply asleep that it would take physical pain or a massive disaster to wake me up. Also, working any kind of magic requires absolute focus, which is difficult to obtain when the person sitting directly next to you will. Not. Stop. Talking.

"Detective," I said quietly, trying to hide my growing irritation. Detective Cara Kane paused in the middle of her tirade and swiveled in her chair to look at me, one of her long legs crossed over the other. She cocked her head like an inquizitive pigeon.

"Hmm?"

"Please stop talking." She arched one dark brow but stopped talking, making a courteous "go ahead" motion in my general direction. I turned back to the map sprawled out in front of me, my hands placed flat on the dark lines of the city's grid. With quiet, it was much easier to concentrate. I closed my eyes and tugged gently on my magic, letting it slip through my fingers like a dog leash. It was centered somewhere around my heart, in my chest somewhere, tucked behind my collarbones. Or at least, that's what it felt like. Really my magic was everywhere, running through my veins with my blood. It warmed my fingers as I sought the signature I had been told to look for. I heard Cara mutter "Purple," so I knew the glow must be spreading around my fingers. My magic filled the grid, snaking down alleys and filling empty tunnels beneath the city. There was a taste of something familiar in an empty warehouse. I pushed harder and gasped as my magic reeled back to me. I cracked my eyes open, only to flinch back as my vision filled with the Detective's face. Cara leaned back slowly.

"You make me nervous when you do that," she grumbled, but there was a reluctant smile on her lips. She pulled the map toward her on the polished surface of the table. One spot was glowing, a dark purple dot pulsing in the warehouse district. By the time I stood, albeit shakily, Cara was already passing the map to the uniformed officers standing at the door, waiting patiently for me to finish my work.

"Can I go?" I asked. I already knew what the answer was going to be, but I had to ask, on the very off chance that she would change her mind this time; it was a matter of principle. Not this time.

Cara sighed darkly. "No. We go through this every time."

I reached for my sweatshirt, tugging the soft material over my head, rearranging the hood so that it didn't pull on my short ponytail. It was right at that length where it was a nuisance if I didn't pull it back, but it wasn't really a ponytail. More like a foxtail, short and bushy.

"Yeah, well, I have to tell you to be quiet so I can concentrate every time too, so I guess we're even," I shot back. Over the hoodie went a black leather jacket. The shakes that accompanied using magic always made me feel like I was freezing to death from the inside out. Cara knew that very well; she handed me a thermos of hot chocolate, like she was rewarding a puppy for a well performed trick. I accepted it with a miffed thank you and guzzled a few swallows. The warmth burned the back of my tongue and throat, just shy of being painful.

"What am I even here for, if I can't ever leave the station or go out in the field? A bloodhound can do the same thing that I can."

"Not as fast or as well, and you know it. Besides. Who needs a bloodhound when I have an enchantress?" Cara picked up the manila file folder and closed it. Now that the uniformed officers had the location of their man, who was a suspect in the armed robbery of a nearby gas station, all we had to do was wait. I sat back down in my chair with a discontent grumble, nursing my hot chocolate, and settled down to wait.

"Scandal, wake up." When I didn't move, Cara shook me more insistently. "Now, Scandal, or you'll miss it. Don't make me pinch you."

That got me up in a hurry. When Cara pinched you, it left a mark. Not a little pink mark that faded in less than an hour, but distinct nail marks, surrounded by a dark bruise that ranged from the size of a dime to a quarter, depending on the pinch. Unfortunately, I had a lot of experience with her pinches. I knew she loved me anyway, but she had a funny way of showing it. The room we were in was almost entirely glass. There was a great view of the front doors, so we had a great view when the uniformed officers brought in the suspect, whom I recognized from the pictures in his file. His hands were cuffed behind his back, his shoulders hunched and head lowered to stare at the tiles. Cara opened the glass door into the hallway, tugging me along by my sleeve.

"And another one bites the dust," one of the officers said cheerfully.

Cara patted my arm proudly. "And it's all because of Scandal here."

The criminal glared, the cops congratulated me on a job well done, and that was the end of another day at the office.

Cara drove me back to my apartment and climbed all three sets of stairs to the front door. My still shaky fingers couldn't fit the key into the lock, so Cara intervened and did it for me. I stumbled inside and dumped my bag on the floor, then flopped face first onto the couch. The door didn't close, which meant that Cara hadn't left yet. I rolled over reluctantly, squinting balefully out of one eye. She was watching me, her fingers twitching. If I didn't know better, I would have said that she was nervous, but it was more likely that our shared social awkwardness was kicking in and she just didn't feel like sharing her feelings.

"You did well today. Get some rest so you can do it again tomorrow. Do you need anything before I go?"

I shook my head and buried my head in the crook of my arm. I still needed another hour or so of sleep before I would be back to full strength. I couldn't get that amount of sleep, or any amount for that matter, while she was here. Her motherly obligations complete, I heard the door close behind her, the lock clicking as she locked it behind her with the spare key. I didn't feel like getting up to flip the deadbolt, so I buried my face in my arm once more, rolled onto my side, and eased myself into a magic induced sleep.

I woke up two hours later, so I wasn't far off on the sleep requirement. I took off my jacket and switched my jeans for a pair of black pajama pants with pockets and blue and purple paw print designs. A text had come in while I was asleep; the owner of a local dog rescue, with a plea for help with a lost dog. That I was a sorceress was a loosely held secret, if that made any sense. Few knew about my magic, and I didn't go out of my way to increase that number, but those who did discussed it openly. I had helped out with finding lost dogs and cats a few times in the past. I didn't mind. Most of the time, the animals on the posters were found long before news ever reached me. If it did, then the situation was dire.

I was starving, but this wouldn't take long. With a dark sigh, I put my pants and jacket back on, although I switched out the boots I was wearing for a comfortable pair of tennis shoes in case I needed to do a lot of walking. I grabbed a handful of snickerdoodles from the jar on my counter, then pulled a handful of maps from a bin in my cupboard, spreading out the one nearest to the area I needed to search. My magic gathered in my fingertips and spread through the map, once more twisting through the city streets. Although I was only seventeen and officially a ward of the state because of my… ahem… past, I was allowed to live alone. Therefore, I could come and go as I pleased. A purple dot had already appeared; I took a celebratory bite of cookie as I grabbed my keys from their peg by the door. The text dinged as it sent, and I headed out the door and down the stairs to do my last good deed of the day.

I jogged down the stairs, folding the map and placing it in my pocket. Now that I was out of the apartment and in the streets, it was easier to follow the trail of my magic. Tracking animals had always been easier for me. They were simpler creatures. Everything about them was visible: how they looked, how they felt, who they loved. They had no secrets, so it was pathetically easy to track them down; all I had to do was seek out the strongest sense that I could find. Add to that the fact that I had worked with this particular dog before. Her owners lived a few blocks away, and we often passed each other on our daily walks. How she'd gone missing I wasn't sure, but all I had to do was follow the trail of magic. I could even walk her home, since I knew where she lived.

The magic led me to an alley on the other side of the city. I was glad that I'd chosen to wear sensible shoes, and sorry now that I hadn't eaten more. I turned into the alley, gripping my keys tightly. It wasn't exactly a dangerous neighborhood, but walking down a dead end alley in the city was never a smart plan, especially as the sun sank lower, casting ominous shadows on everything crouching in the alley. I was pretty sure that I could take care of myself in any situation, but I wasn't going to push my luck.

My magic cooled, slowing to a trickle as I crept around

the side of a filthy garbage can. I couldn't see any animal, or at least not one that I wanted to see. I refused to see any of the smaller, grimier variety.

"Come on out, Moon," I said softly. I crouched down to see the eyes under the trash can, trying not to think about what was on the ground and therefore staining my jeans right now. Ever so slowly, Moon crept out. I sat, allowing her to crawl into my lap. She was a tiny, fluffy little creature with black spots, but she was so filthy that she looked all black. Her collar was dangling loosely from her neck, the tags half obscured by the scum that she had collected during her most recent adventure. She didn't seem to be hurt, but it was hard to tell with her curled up against my chest and refusing to budge. Standing up while holding her was a challenge, mostly because it was throwing off my balance, and I couldn't put my hand down to help. She nuzzled against my neck, and I fought not to squirm as a bit of sludge flipped against my neck. With my magic I could have cleaned her up in the blink of an eye but tracking her down had pretty well decimated my last reserves. It didn't take much to track her but having to follow it all the way across the city, after what I'd already used today, was difficult. I also didn't want to be completely without magic, just in case something came up later. Cara would not be happy if we caught a case and her partner the sorceress didn't have any magic to use.

Moon lived in a nice, upscale brick building with a wrought iron gate and steep concrete steps leading up to the front door. A golden gargoyle knocker rested against the heavy wood and I raised it slowly, trying not to startle Moon too badly with the noise. I could just see me, trying to be the conquering hero by bringing her back to her family, only to have them open the door on me wrestling with a tiny, muddy dog on their front porch. That would ruin the mystique just a little bit.

Fortunately, Moon seemed to recognize that she was home. She yipped playfully, her plumy tail smacking my arm as she strained to reach the door. It opened, and the older woman on the other side gasped, her wrinkled hands flying to her mouth.

"Ernest, come here!" She wore an argyle sweater and an expensive looking string of pearls, along with brown corduroy pants and soft flats. Everything about this place seemed very upscale, which is why it was such a surprise for me that I had found their dog wandering loose. Not to mention the fact that she must have been gone some time to have caught the attention of the animal rescue group that had contacted me. It was a strange situation.

"Oh, my goodness. Thank you so much! Come here, baby," the woman cooed, holding her hands out for Moon. I stepped closer to hand her over, but Moon had other ideas; she took a flying leap into the older lady's arms, and I winced at the wet splat from the mud in her coat. That sweater probably cost more than a month of my rent, and I did not foresee the wet dog mud coming out easily. She didn't seem to care.

"Oh, baby, where have you been?" She cuddled the pup tightly and I stepped back, trying to give them some privacy. She grabbed my arm, tugging gently as she smiled.

"I'm terribly sorry for the hullabaloo. I've just missed our little girl so much." I smiled at the old-fashioned phrasing. It was almost as cute as the fact that this classy lady was cuddling a muddy dog and holding onto my jacket, which was arguably just as gross from holding her on the walk back.

Add to that the fact that I hadn't showered after work today, and I was probably pretty rank.

"It's no problem at all. It's just nice to see that you care about your pet." As I spoke, an older man shuffled in from the next room, wearing an old robe and fumbling with a pair of gold-rimmed eyeglasses.

"What is it, darling?" he asked, then broke into a huge grin when he saw Moon. She yipped and licked his face. The couple played with their dog, and I shuffled back a step, wanting to leave them alone but not wanting to yank my arm out of the lady's grip.

"I'll leave you to it."

"Oh, no, you must stay for supper. It's the least we can do after you brought our beloved back to us."

Oh, no. Good deeds were all well and good, but I'd had about enough of magic for the day, and I was definitely ready for a shower. Socializing with the upper crust was not going to improve the day. "Really, it's not necessary. I just wanted to help out." She had finally released my arm and I shifted back; my badge glinted, and Ernest's eyes widened. He smiled knowingly.

"I see. I was wondering how you found her. I see we have our answer."

I glanced down, pulling my jacket forward to hide it, but the damage was already done. I sighed softly and held out my hand after wiping it off on my jeans. Ernest didn't seem to mind the sludge. "Yes, sir. I'm Scandal Becker. I work for the Sorcery Division."

Ernest smiled at his wife, one arm in the crook of her elbow. "Darling, I think Scandal would like to get home, and we wouldn't want to keep her. Perhaps she'll come back some other time?" His eyes twinkled warmly, and I grinned back. I didn't really know him or his wife, but the fact that he was giving me an out was enough of a reason for me to like him. His wife's politeness and seeming inattention to the fact that she was holding a dog with enough mud on it to be a small golem made me like her just as much.

"Yes, sir. Another time, when there's less going on. I just wanted to make sure that Moon got back to you safely."

"Well, we're glad that you did. If you ever need anything, anything at all, just reach out. We'll do whatever we can to help."

I smiled. "Thank you. I appreciate that." Little did I know then that I would have to cash that chip in sooner than I thought.

Chapter Two

Buzz. I slapped my alarm clock sleepily, with rising aggression, but it took me a few minutes to realize that it wasn't going off. The noise was my cell phone. The light on the screen flashed blue with a waiting text message. I fumbled for it with my free hand, and tumbled out of the bed, taking half of my covers with me. I took a deep breath and grabbed the phone, squinting balefully at the tiny letters of the screen.

Get up. We caught a case. I'll be there in ten minutes.

"Surprise, surprise," I muttered under my breath. I flung my covers aside, or at least tried to. It took me a few moments to untangle myself, only to pull them back slowly when a dark mark caught my eye. Not just one, but ten, blackish purple marks seared into my bed sheet, in the shape of my fingerprints. They were so well defined that I could see the ridges and whorls, as well as the scar on the pad of my left thumb, tucked on the underside of the bottom sheet. I sighed darkly. Yet another set of sheets with these marks. When I was asleep, I didn't have control over my magic. Typically that wasn't a problem, but when I had nightmares, it was. I had a cuff that dampened my magic, but I hadn't worn it for quite some time. It looked like that would soon have to change, at least if this continued.

Ten minutes wasn't a lot of time to get ready. With a new case heading my way, I decided to dress more for function than fashion. I slipped on a pair of skinny jeans and a pair of short black boots, then a hunter green top that bared a few inches of my midriff. The cuff lay on my bedside table, shoved as far back as it could be while still residing on the table. To me, it looked smug. I made a face at it and grabbed a silver arrow necklace instead. On the top went a jean jacket, and I was dressed. The microwave beeped the message that my breakfast burrito was ready when there was an insistent honk from the street below. Juggling the steaming hot morning meal between my palms with soft hisses of pain, I tossed the strap of my messenger bag over my shoulder and headed out the door to work.

Cara was oddly quiet on the drive to the station. No matter how much I pestered her, she wouldn't give me a straight answer as to what was bothering her.

"Enough, Scandal!" she burst out finally. "I am under strict orders not to tell you anything until we get to the station and then I can hand it off to someone who knows a whole lot more than I do about the situation. So please just be quiet for the next ten minutes." She slapped the steering wheel with the palm of her hand in frustration.

"Fine," I seethed. Fuming, I plugged in my earbuds and cranked up the music up, staring out the window with typical teenage angst. The pop music was low enough that I could have heard Cara if she had chosen to speak, but she didn't. She pulled the nondescript police vehicle into the parking garage next to the space, nosing it into one of the spaces on the lowest levels reserved for detectives. The signs in front of each dictated which division could park there. Homicide and narcotics were listed, but Cara pulled into the one with a tall metal sign that said "Reserved for Detectives: Sorcery Division." The symbol on the sign matched the one on our badges. Mine was clipped to my belt. The badge was iron, a heavy star with a rainbow of colors backing it. Mine had a purple bar under it, to indicate the color of my magic. Cara's lacked that bar, although everything else about the badge was the same. We climbed out our respective sides and headed in the automatic front doors.

The room that we spent our days in was essentially a giant aquarium, all four sides entirely glass, with taupe blinds dangling to the floor. There were only a few of these rooms in the whole station. They were commonly known as "magic rooms" and were specifically assigned to the sorcerers who worked for the department, one for each of us. There were only four of us. I hadn't really been hired. More like reluctantly recruited.

I tugged my earbuds out and crossed my arms across my chest. There were three people already in the room, two seated and the chief standing in the corner. I went warily to my leather chair at the head of the table and sat down. My magic sparked around my fingers, a halo of violet flickering around my fingertips. With a smile, the younger of the two men seated raised his hand also, elbow flat on the table as he offered his hand. Our palms touched. The two colors of our magic flowed together. Warmth flowed up my arm like warm water in reverse. The boy's grin widened, and we stayed like that, hands clasped and multicolored magic swirling up our arms, until the chief cleared his throat. That touch had told me quite a bit about this boy, or at least his magic.

"Scandal, this is Rift. Rift, Scandal." As much as I wanted to, I didn't offer to shake his hand again. Rift's eyes were clear green in the bright room, like stained glass lit from above. He ran his long fingers through the thick, honey gold hair that fell into his face. It was trimmed shorter on the sides and long on the top, falling into his face. He was wearing a jean jacket also, with a black tee and faded jeans. The look was casual, but more than that, it was how someone my age would dress. It was a far cry from the long trench coats and somber clothing of the older, more experienced sorcerers.

"Not that I'm complaining, but what are you doing here? It's nice to have another sorcerer around, don't get me wrong, especially one that was born in the same decade as me."

"I heard that," one of the sorcerers piped up. One of the aforementioned trench coats who happened to be walking by, on the way to his own magic room.

"I know," I said easily. He just grinned and kept walking, shaking his head. Rift watched the exchange, his full lips twitching.

"I know about as much as you do, I think. Why don't we ask our partners, since they seem to be in the know?" We had moved to stand shoulder to shoulder. So had Cara and Rift's partner, a bulky man built like a football player, the shoulders of his suit jacket straining to contain him. He was by no means a small man, but he seemed to be in good shape. Rift and I looked at the two of them, they looked at the chief, and the chief slapped a file down on the table with an irritated sigh. The other detective, who had introduced himself as Special Agent Elliott Roth, snagged the file before any of us had taken a step to reach it. After a cursory examination, he passed it onto Cara, and so it went.

I raised my hand, feeling very much like a preschooler. Rift's presence was making me take a hard look at my manners, which might not have been a bad thing. "No offense, but why are they here? It only takes one sorcerer to cast a tracking spell."

"None taken," Rift assured me.

The chief conceded with a nod. "Yes, but this man isn't your typical petty criminal. He's known only as Edgar, and he sells magical artifacts on the black market."

"I understand, but I agree with Scandal. This is a job for one sorcerer, and I think Scandal is more than capable of working a tracking spell. Why am I here?" As he spoke, Rift glanced sideways at me, cheeks flushed. The way his head was tilted, those long blond locks slipped into his face. It was a shy gesture, one that I hadn't expected from him.

The chief sighed darkly, looking to our respective partners for help; both shrugged helplessly.

"Teenagers," he muttered, and my ears perked up. If the chief, who likely knew all of our ages, called us both teenagers, then that meant that Rift had to be at least close to my age. "So impatient. You need to be here because Edgar has an artifact that prevents him from being tracked. The best solution we could come up with was to build a magical barrier to keep him in the city, and you two are the best we can find for that task."

"Are you even sure that he's still in the city? It wouldn't make much sense for us to work the spell, only for him to be in Miami or something."

"As of a few hours ago, he was still in the city. That's why we need you to perform the spell as quickly as possible."

I glanced at Rift, who had an identical startled look. I'd

never even attempted something like this before, and from the look on his face, Rift hadn't either.

"Are you sure we can? I mean, I don't know about Scandal, but I haven't done anything past tracking and warming spells for, like, a year at least. Let alone something as big as this." He made a vague gesture.

I nodded. I wasn't offended because I'd been following that same train of thought. Tracking spells were how I spent most of my days, tracking down suspects that had fled or people who had jumped bail. At most I used the occasional warming spell. Nothing like the amount of power it would take to build a shield around an entire city of millions of people, one that would block this one specific person from leaving, no matter the method. On top of that the spell had to allow everyone else to pass through, so as not to raise suspicion.

"We have faith in you two."

Rift squared his shoulders. "All right. I'm game to try it if Scandal is." I nodded, and there were audible sighs of relief from the three adults.

"What do you need from us?"

"Do you have anything of his? Anything that he has touched or handled?" They all three stared at me like I had taken leave of my senses; I sighed gustily. "Fine. His file then, and videos or pictures. Anything we can use to start getting a feel for him, so that we can weave it into the spell."

Soon the table was filled with files, covered with black and white surveillance photos of the same man. He was of medium height and fit, with short hair and a devilish goatee. In each photo, he carried a briefcase, and a thick amulet dangled from around his neck. Unless I missed my guess, that amulet was the talisman that shielded him from tracking spells. If we could get it away from him, we wouldn't have any problem tracking him from now on. We had to find him first.

That's where Cara and Special Agent Elliott came in. While Rift and I sorted through the photos with magic in our fingers, Cara and Elliott settled in for some good old fashioned police work. I sipped hot chocolate and listened to Cara make a call to a confidential informant, then flip through a few more witness statements.

"I think we're good," Rift said finally. He sat back in his chair and ran his long fingers through his hair.

"But I need something to eat before I even think about trying something like this." He raised his cup and swirled it; liquid sloshed inside. "Plus, my coffee is cold."

I nodded in agreement. "Ditto for the hot chocolate." I raised the nearly empty cup in salute. "Do you want to get some lunch before we get started?" Cara and Elliott had left about half an hour ago to run down some leads. Rift and I had stayed behind to finish building our "profile", which would allow us to build a shield that would soon become a net. It would be a massive undertaking that would no doubt take hours, if not days, to complete. Not to mention that one of us would have to pour magic into the shield constantly, for fear of it collapsing and allowing Edgar to escape.

Rift frowned thoughtfully. "Of course, I'd love to, I'm starving, but is there anywhere around here?"

I nodded and grabbed my jacket from the back of my chair, sliding it on as I grabbed my messenger bag. It went everywhere with me, including my favorite Mom-and-Pop diner, it was just around the corner. I scrawled a quick note to our overzealous partners before we headed out of the magic room. By wordless, unanimous decision, we took the stairs rather than the elevator. When we had been seated, Rift's long legs and athletic build made it seem like he would be much bigger than me, but I was only about an inch shorter, although much lankier. We took the steps two at a time, buttoning our jackets as we headed out the front doors. Rather than turning left, toward the station's parking garage, I led Rift to the right and around the corner. A few blocks away was my favorite hole in the wall, a family owned diner tucked between a bookstore and an alternative church. I held the door open for Rift and he stepped in, turning his head to get a better view.

The moment we stepped across the threshold, there was a sound of shattering glass and a startled shout. Both of us spun, magic on our fingers; Gina, one of the owners' daughters was already bending down by the bar to clean up the stack of dirty plates she had dropped, cheeks flaming. I crouched to help and Rift did as well, placing a hand gently on my shoulder to steady himself as he wobbled on his heels. We picked up the shards, careful not to cut ourselves on the sharp edges. Somehow, it seemed like only only one of the plates had shattered, which was a small miracle in itself.

"Are you okay, Gina?" She nodded emphatically, looking anywhere but at Rift. I smiled understandingly at her, which only deepened her blush. I could see where she was coming from. Rift was very attractive, which I was doing my best not to notice, at least until this massive magical undertaking was behind us. I didn't have the energy to do both, and we both needed all the focus we could muster for something like this. I didn't date often; not for lack of trying, but more because most people, male or female, didn't want to date a sorceress. Bad breakups are messy enough without worrying that your ex is going to get their revenge by turning you into a pigeon, I guess.

"Do you want me to…" I trailed off. Not wanting to draw too much attention but wanting to offer my help, I wiggled my fingers, glowing faintly violet. Gina glanced over her shoulder through the kitchen window, craning her neck to see upward, to see where her father was flipping pancakes in a cast iron skillet.

"Yes, please," she murmured shyly. A soft violet glow emanated from my fingers and enveloped the glass shards; they fit back together seamlessly. I lifted the plate up to my face and turned it over to search for cracks or flaws. Finding none, I handed it back.

"Thank you." Gina took the plate, placed it on the tall stack of plates, and hurried into the kitchen.

"Well, that was odd," Rift remarked as we seated ourselves. He opened one of the plastic coated menus to peruse it, but I didn't bother. When Gina came back, still refusing to look at Rift despite his earnest smile, I ordered with the ease of practice.

"Chocolate chip pancakes, scrambled eggs, and sausage links, please."

"And your hot chocolate?" she confirmed. I nodded. I had almost forgotten, probably from either nerves or the fact that I had a companion, when I usually ate alone. Actually, I usually had to order something to go, if I even came to find something other than vending machine food in the first place. It was a refreshing change to be able to sit down and eat, that I could take my time. The fact that I had a companion for once was a surprise, but a welcome one. Now, if we had time to eat the whole meal before our partners came back and made us perform a work of enchantment that would no doubt knock us out for a week after we finished it, then it would be a minor miracle. Second only to pigs peeking in the windows of a passenger airliner.

"And for you?" Gina asked, finally looking at Rift, albeit slightly above his left shoulder in order to avoid eye contact. To me that had seen her every day since I had moved to this neighborhood, she was impressed by Rift's attractiveness but trying to stay professional. I didn't blame her.

"I'll take the sourdough French toast and the shredded hash browns. Hazelnut coffee, too, if you have it. Please and thank you."

Gina scratched his order into her little notebook and hurried away. He rested his elbows on the table and leaned forward.

"So, Scandal. I don't know any more about you than you do about me, so why don't we get to know one another a little better? How did you start working for the department?"

"What, didn't you read a dossier on me?" I teased, dodging the question. While I wasn't exactly ashamed of how I had come to work for local law enforcement, it wasn't exactly the kind of thing that would inspire trust in me, either. I didn't want to sabotage a potentially very fruitful relationship with my less-than-stellar past. He raised his eyebrows.

"Since you're clearly avoiding that particular topic, how about this: we each get to ask the other questions. If we don't want to answer the question, all we have to do is say pass, no questions asked. Deal?"

He reached across the table to shake hands, nudging a syrup bottle out of the way with his elbow. I took it, shaking firmly. His grip was warm and soft, calluses on his fingers.

"Deal. My turn to ask a question. You're my age, probably about seventeen. I work for a podunk little police force, but you work for the federal government. How did you get pulled in?"

"I almost burned down my school with magefire," he said matter of factly, and my eyes widened. Magefire was a wall of magical flame that devoured everything in its path and could not be extinguished by any conventional means. It could only be put out by the person who started it or an extremely powerful magic user. I'd had a few encounters with magefire before, and I could say with absolute certainty that if an out of control young warlock had accidentally unleashed it in a school full of kids, unable to stop it, hundreds could have died before someone could be found who was able to stop it. In other words, far worse than what I had done.

"Oh," I said faintly. I picked at a tear in the red vinyl of the booth's red and white bench seat, but Rift picked up the conversation like what he had just admitted wasn't a life changing secret. He answered nearly all of my questions, studying the diner curiously all the while. It was a mixture of an old style soda shop slash diner and a poetry slam. Red and white vinyl booths and formica table tops on sturdy silver legs hinted at the diner vibe, while dark, convoluted chandeliers barely lit the darkness. There was a small stage near the front with a short microphone. Coat racks jutted from the end of each booth, including ours. Our jean jackets hung there, his dark and mine faded.

Overall, Rift was more forthcoming in answering questions than I was with answering his. We both avoided questions about our families and had to sort of feel each other out. If one of us didn't want to talk about a particular subject, it was a safe bet to assume that the other one didn't either, so we nosed around sensitive topics like a sniffing dog before slinking away. I had no idea how long we sat there, eating our breakfast and laughing at each other's progressively sillier questions, before the first text from Cara dinged onto my phone screen.

Done chasing down leads for now. Meet back at the station ASAP.

I showed the text to Rift, but neither of us were anxious to leave. Ten minutes later, another ding.

Get your butt back here NOW. We need to start now.

Just a few minutes had passed when the third text came in, perfectly coinciding with Rift's text from his handler.

If you're not back here in five minutes we're coming to get you.

Rift and I locked eyes, then hurriedly grabbed our jackets.

"I don't know about you, but I'm not exactly eager to face the wrath of the overprotective parent slash partner," Rift said. We had already discussed, or rather had a spirited argument about, who would pay while we ate. I dug out my wallet and put down the money for my meal; Rift laid down enough for his meal and the tip.

I agreed with him reluctantly, swinging my jacket on. "About as eager as I am to attempt a gigantic spell that will almost certainly knock us out for about a week."

As predicted, our partners were not happy with our little lunch da-outing. "Where were you?" Cara snapped, Her voice was about a step below a shout and I cringed inwardly; Rift's hand nudged mine, our bony knuckles brushing together briefly.

"We were gathering our strength," he responded. Cara was an imposing woman, tall and fierce, especially when she was looming over us. Rift lifted his head, the long strands of his hair shifting. "You have no concept of how much energy this is going to cost us." He crossed his arms as he spoke, still meeting Cara's glare squarely. "You ask so much of us, and never stop to consider how vulnerable it makes us feel, that we're going to put all of our magic, our energy into something, without anything left to protect ourselves with. Maybe if we pass out up there, then you'll get it." His partner shot him a warning glare, which I caught out of the corner of my eye as I snatched up the map and headed for the door. We'd decided to start the spell on the roof. The fewer walls and ceilings between us and the shield we were trying to build, the easier it would be for us and the less magic that it would take. Not to mention the extra space that it would give us to work. This way, we could see if the spell was working and make any necessary adjustments to the working. One would build the spell until they needed to take a break, which is when the other would take over. Whoever wasn't building the spell would stand back and watch, making small adjustments as needed. Rift and I jogged up the stairs, then opened the door and stepped into the fresh air, or as fresh as city air could be.

Gravel crunched beneath my sneakers. A sort of covered pavilion had been set up since this morning, anchored deep in the shifting gravel. Ominous gray clouds were building all around the city, split here and there by blinding white gashes of lightning. The gusts of wind blew my straight black hair into my eyes as I squinted at the sky; a few strands had pulled loose of my ponytail and were making themselves troublesome. There had been no sign of rain when I'd left my apartment this morning, nor on the weather report last night. I could only hope that the bad weather was a fluke of nature and not a sign that this venture was doomed before we had even begun.

I ducked under the flap of the tent and held it up for Rift to come through also. Our partners were probably still panting up the stairs. They were both fit, or at least Elliott seemed to be and I knew Cara was, but that many stairs can take a toll on anyone. The pavilion was completely covered, with the side facing the city rolled up and tied tightly. Rift unrolled our map on the table that had been set up, weighted down in the corners with stones as it flapped with each intermittent gust of strong wind. A few chairs had been set up; there were two cots situated at the back, about an inch from one of the fabric walls. A box of snacks and a few bottles of water were tucked beneath the table that the map was on. While Rift was readying himself and our equipment, I did too. My hair had now come almost entirely out of its ponytail, so I rolled my sleeves up to my elbows and pulled it back into a ponytail so that it wasn't blowing in my face every time the wind gusted. Rift probably wanted to do the same, but even the longest of his hair wasn't long enough to pull back. The last thing I did was take off all of my jewelry. Cara had given all of it to me to dampen my power, to make it easier to control. It wasn't impossible to work magic with it on, but it was easier if I wasn't bound by all of it. Besides, I was going to need all that magic that I could muster for this, and even that might not be enough. Onto the surface of the table went a stack of layered gold necklaces, a few pairs of earrings from my three sets of piercings, two rings, a ton of bangles, and, as Rift watched with wide eyes, I pulled my pants leg up and added a silver anklet to the glittering pile. Rift made his own neat pile directly next to it, a silver ring and a set of clanking dog tags that looked perfectly normal, but if I looked at them out of the corner of my eye, they shone acid green, like they were radioactive. His magic shimmered pale turquoise, which meant that someone else had enchanted the jewelry for his use. My jewelry had been enchanted by different people; there were slivers of pink, maroon, teal, and forest green in the mix, different from my own varying shades of purple. Some sorcerers had a favorite talisman maker, like one would have a favorite jeweler or tailor, but they were still rare enough that it was sometimes necessary to use more than one maker. They were typically sorcerers gifted with crafting in some way, whether it be finding crystals or simply weaving an enchantment around an existing object, and hard to find. Hard enough that it was odd that all of the enchanted jewelry he had was all made by the same person.

Perhaps his jewelry was to make it easier for him to control his magic? Some of mine was that way, a bracelet and one of the pairs of earrings, but most of them were containers that I stored my magic in for later use. If I didn't, the excess power clawed at my skin, to the point of being physically painful. Judging by the charms that he wore, Rift had the opposite problem.

"So now it's my turn," I said grimly, and Rift nodded. Our brunch break hadn't been entirely for fun. We'd decided that I would start the working and that he would feed me power until I got too tired to continue, then we'd switch places. Working magic wasn't like following a recipe; it was more like building something, pouring magic through the pattern and hoping the extra power didn't snap back at you like a whip or a tree branch in a strong wind.

I took a deep breath and placed the tips of my fingers on the map, nudging our charms to the side in case I needed them later, careful not to knock them off the table. My magic was almost fully recovered from yesterday; it leapt eagerly to my command. I started to build the spell, first raising it around the city like a dome, then making it impenetrable to only one. Glittering lines appeared in front of my closed eyes like a circuit board. The innate magic of the city pushed back at my grip. As any large city did, it gathered magic at strong focal points, like the landmarks that tourists and locals alike gawked at every day, rain or shine. Not only the magic of sorcerers and sorceresses, but also the innate power of every living being, from the most affluent congressman to the peskiest pigeon winging high above our heads. So much power didn't want to be contained, especially not by the likes of me, a teenage sorceress who had no business fooling around with this much power. I was already struggling, and I had only just begun. It was a difficult working, so I threw myself into it with all my concentration.

I released my magic with a stuttering gasp, my weak knees giving way beneath me. I would have fallen to the gravel if not for the wooden chair that appeared behind my knees, just in time for me to fold into it. I was shivering uncontrollably as Cara pulled my sleeves down and gently draped a thick sherpa blanket around my shoulders, but there was a trail of warmth on the lower half of my face. I reached up to touch it; the tips of my fingers came away wet and warm, the same warm blood that was still dripping from my nose and down my chin. Through the haze of exhaustion and shivering, I heard Cara ask the other people on the roof if anyone had a tissue as I tilted my head back. There was an emptiness in my body where my magic should have been, down to my soul, but I gathered up what was left and grabbed Rift's hand. He jolted, and my vision flashed blue and purple as our magics melded. We both straightened as the power mixed. It felt odd to have both his power and mine running through my veins. Mine was warm and familiar, whereas his felt like sparks popping beneath my skin. I took my time settling in, and then joined Rift in the working.

I had built the bare bones, and he was fleshing them out. What had taken the most out of me wasn't building the shield; that was almost easy. The hard part was allowing everyone but Edgar to come and go as they pleased, which meant that we had to inspect each person's aura and rework the spell around them. Each person's aura was as unique as their fingerprint or DNA, a product of their experiences and the magic that they had soaked up throughout their life. Complicating matters was the fact that we didn't know what Edgar's aura felt like, so we had to be sure that we didn't free his aura by accident in our haste. I could immediately discount anyone female or too young, but we had no way of knowing how old was too old to knock out; the process was time consuming. It was also complex, and that was what had sapped my strength. With Rift and I combining our energy, I felt better, if a little weak. Unfortunately, Rift's magic was a temporary crutch, and I knew it. Once we separated, I would be more drained than ever. It was like a sugar high. For a little while, you felt fresh and energized, right before the crash came and your energy took a nosedive. I wasn't at that point yet, probably because I was helping Rift control his magic, sharing the power and the pressure. For all that, Rift was the one leading, and he was the one who found the suspicious aura.

I felt a gentle tug on my magic, like he was pulling on my hand to get my attention. I was only vaguely aware of my physical body, even our clasped hands, but I knew neither of us had moved. I followed Rift's blue light to a dark aura. Not dark in an ominous way; more like there was no aura there at all, like it was being hidden from our sight. It was slippery and slimy, like wet spaghetti noodles, not to mention how it seemed to be bouncing around the city. I say seemed because it was actually entirely still, which I only figured out once I got a grip on the shadowy aura and was able to ignore the phantoms. I could feel Rift tiring, his magic strained by the pursuit and the spell. I disentangled myself from him and chased the odd aura. No matter how hard I tried, I couldn't pin it down.

Someone pinched me. Then again, and it was definitely not in my magic this time. The sudden, unexpected pain dragged me out of what little magic I had left. A third, totally unnecessary pinch, and I had ripped my arm away from Cara before my eyes were even open. "Could you not? 'Cause that'd be great."

"What are you even doing?" That was Rift, and I had to look around for a second before I realized that he was right next to me, kneeling next to my chair. We were still holding hands and he was leaning on my legs. I expected to want to let go, but I didn't. I expected to be so exhausted that I couldn't see straight, but I felt weirdly energized, like the sparks of Rift's energy were keeping me up.

Rift didn't seem ready to let go of my hand either. When I'd gone back into the working with him, I'd been sitting in the chair and he had been a few steps in front of me, holding hands. Now he was kneeling next to me, his back braced against the outside of my thigh, and our long fingers were woven together.

The chief was arguing spiritedly with Special Agent Elliott and Cara left our side to join the quarrel.

"So that happened."

"Yeah." We paused for a moment to reflect on what we

had seen in the working and then said together, "Have you ever seen anything like it?" Rift flushed darkly. He was on his knees facing me now, one of his hands balanced on my knee. He was watching me carefully, waiting to see if I wanted him to let go, but when I didn't say anything, he continued.

"You first."

I couldn't help but smile. "No, I haven't seen anything like it before, but it must have been that Edgar guy. I can't think of anything else or anyone else that it could have been."

"Me neither."

The raised voices were finally loud enough to penetrate our deep concentration, too loud to ignore without concerted effort. I twisted around to look at the arguing agents. I stood slowly, expecting to fall over almost immediately. Not even close.

"Is it just me, or…" Rift trailed off. His bangs tickled his forehead as he studied the backs of his hands, then his palms.

"Do I feel oddly strong and not at all like I'm about to pass out, like I usually do?" I provided.

He pointed at me like I'd just won first prize on a game show. "That." His fingertips almost looked singed; mine did as well. Actually, considering the magic that we had just wrought, it was a minor miracle that we hadn't accidentally burned our fingerprints into the map. Now that I really thought about it, I wasn't sure that we hadn't. I sort of wanted to check, but my curiosity over what our superiors were arguing about won out.

"What's going on?" I asked, poking my head over Cara's shoulder. Both her face and Elliott's wore identical unyielding expressions. The chief pointed an accusing finger at me and I stepped back, directly into Cobalt's chest. The chief snorted as we untangled ourselves. I felt better than I usually did after a working of that size, but my skin still felt oddly sensitive. Bumping into Rift made the magic lurch beneath my skin, enough to make my surroundings on the rooftop spin. I locked my legs and brace myself, waiting for the room to stop spinning. Palms on his sharp elbows, Rift hugged himself, but he didn't back away from me.

"They look fine to me. I see no reason why we can't go downstairs and do the briefing right now."

Elliott sighed gustily and Rift whipped his head toward his handler, blond hair flying. "How many times do we have to tell you? They may look okay now, but they're exhausted. They need to get some rest."

Cara jumped in as soon as he stopped to take a breath. I had to hand it to them, they did make a great team. They had the grace of a well oiled machine, and the absolute certainty that came with being handlers of teenage sorcerers for most of their careers. Cara, for instance, had been assigned to me since my...ahem, incident, and I knew that she had been assigned to others before me. Agents assigned to sorcery divisions had to be smart, tough and dang near bombproof. If they so much as blinked when a match lit by itself, they probably wouldn't be able to hack it with the sorcery division. "They're exhausted, and there is nothing more for them to do today anyway. It will all wait until tomorrow. If you push them, you risk losing the use of your two best enchanters." The chief's face reddened, but Cara didn't back down. Clearly the chief didn't appreciate being challenged like that in front of other people, but I think what he disliked the most was the insinuation that Rift and I were the most powerful sorcerers here. Two teenagers, with a whole sorcery unit spread throughout the building, working on other projects. Obviously it rankled him, and did nothing to improve the situation. I made a face at Cara and tried to step in before this escalated any further.

"Don't we get any say in this?" I asked. "After all, it's our body that you're talking about, and our power."

"No!" Cara and Elliott said together. Cara grabbed my arm just above the elbow, and Elliott gripped Rift's. It was Cara's favorite way to manhandle me when she had to get physical. With her hand just above my elbow, I couldn't free myself without flailing around in an undignified way, if I could even get free at all. "We're leaving now." They all but dragged us down the stairs. Cara's grip on my arm was near bruising and tight, like she was trying to hold me up in case I fell. Problem was, I wasn't in any danger of falling. At least, not if they slowed down a little and stopped making me trip on cracks in the sidewalk.

"What is the matter with you? We're fine," I hissed. That stopped Cara, and by extension, everyone else. She gripped my chin and looked me directly in the eyes.

"I've known you for a long time, and I know that after something like that, you're usually unconscious by now. I don't know what's going on, why this time is different, but we're going home and calling the witch doctor." She pointed at Rift, who straightened so quickly that his back cracked. "And you're coming too.

Chapter Three

"One more time: I told you, I'm fine."

"And I'm fine too," Rift confirmed.

Neither Cara nor Elliott seemed convinced. They were both watching us like a hawk while we waited for the doctor to arrive. While most doctors had magic, a few specialized in enchantment-related health issues. The department had one on call for its four sorcerers at all times, and Cara had called her before we left the roof.

"And I told you, I'm not convinced you're not going to pass out any second. As soon as you think you're fine: Boom! Down you go. I don't know why you haven't already."

"Well, I think I might have an idea about that..." I began when I was interrupted by a rap on the door. Rift started to rise to answer it, then sat down at a withering glare from Cara. Elsie, the doctor, followed Cara in. As always, she looked perfectly fashionable and approachable, with just enough sophistication to be a professional. The perfect mixture. She wore a white sundress decorated with cheery sunflowers and white lace up sandals. Her curly blonde hair was pooled around her shoulders, all the way to the small of her back. She placed her bag on the table and opened it, rifling through it with her painted fingernails. The bag was a black leather handbag, much more fashionable than an old fashioned doctor's bag for house calls.

"Hey, Scandal. How's your latest knockout going?"

I winced in embarrassment and Rift glanced at me. I did my best to ignore him. "Hey, Elsie. Actually, I feel perfectly fine. Not like last time." Or every other time before that.

"What happened last time?" Rift asked curiously. Like me, he had bundled up in anticipation of the magic aftermath cold spell, but he had rolled up his sleeves and shed the jean jacket. There was a leather cuff on his right wrist, the only accessory he hadn't taken off, which was good, because we had never retrieved our belongings from the roof. They would still be there in the morning, but still. I wondered what the significance of that particular item was, if it was enchanted or just sentimental.

Elsie opened her mouth to answer, but I pointed at her. "No. We agreed not to discuss that incident in polite company." To Rift I said, "It's nothing we need to discuss." Now or preferably ever.

Elsie held up her hands in surrender. "Fine. Get over here so I can check you out."

I stood and went to stand in front of her; she put her hands on my face. As always, I felt her warm yellow magic, like liquid sunshine, flow through my veins. Unlike usual however, I it caused a blinding pain, as if the magic was ripping me open from the inside out. I cried out and reeled away, stumbling over the edge of the coffee table and crashing hard to the floor. I held out my hands to stop Rift and Elsie from approaching me. Without the excess magic in my system, it didn't hurt anymore. It had drained the extra energy a little, though.

Rift sat down again where he was, a few feet away.

"I think I know what's going on," Elsie began. She touched Rift's arm and he reacted much the same way that I had, although less dramatically because he was already on the floor.

"*Why* would you do that?" he gasped indignantly. He rubbed the veins in his wrist like they were the source of his pain. If it was anything like the pain that I had felt when Elsie's magic had invaded, it wasn't just one spot. It had been all encompassing, like there was nothing in the world other than the pain. His wrist was probably just the easiest. I, for one, knew that the places that I had been injured in the past, like my broken arm, had felt it more than anywhere else. The skin above my elbow was tender, and I could see why Rift was reacting that way, since I felt the aftermath of the magic as pain too.

Elsie pulled over a chair so that she was facing us and crossed her slim legs, far too dignified to sit on the floor with us. Rift scooted over so that he was leaning against the front of the couch next to me.

"Because I think I know what's wrong with you two. Did you mix your magics when you were working the spell?"

Rift nodded. His fingers were tangled in the longer hair at the top of his head, which seemed to be his nervous habit. "We had to. A spell of that size requires too much power for only one enchanter. If we hadn't shared our power, the spell would have fizzled out before it was even close to complete."

"And have either of you ever shared magic with another person before?" I had to think about it. Most of my experience was with tracking spells and the occasional shielding spell, as well as other small magics. I did vaguely remember sharing with other enchanters. This wasn't the first time I had done it, but it was the first time the aftermath had felt like this. Normally I was unconscious at this time after a big working. Instead, I still felt weirdly energetic, like I'd downed an energy drink that hadn't worn off yet.

"No. I've done it before."

"Me too," Rift provided. "Quite a few times, actually. It's never felt like this before."

"One more question, or rather an order. Try to use magic, without touching each other."

I sighed and willed a ball of light to appear in my palm. To my shock, it was not my deep violet, but rather a shining turquoise. Rift tried the same spell, with the exact same result.

Elsie smiled smugly. Both Elliott and Cara came to watch, staring at the mismatched flames in our hands.

"That's trippy," Elliott muttered, and there were nods all around. I closed my fingers, extinguishing the turquoise light hovering over my palm.

"So what's the prognosis, Doc?"

Elsie frowned briefly. "I've never seen anything like it before. As best as I can tell, you two somehow managed to 'give' each other magic. The unfamiliar gift is what's keeping you awake, like a shot of adrenaline."

I nodded slowly. "I follow you so far. But why would it have hurt so much when your magic was introduced? It should have had the same effect, right?"

Elsie made a maybe, maybe not gesture with her hand. "Sometimes another person's magic mixes better with your own. Not to mention that with Rift's magic and your own already in your system, mine was just one thing too many. Your system just couldn't handle it."

"So what do we do?" Rift asked. He hadn't ended his spell and was playing with the violet light in his long fingers. "Right now I feel fine, but I would like to sleep sometime in this lifetime."

I raised my hand, feeling like a preschooler asking for a second snack at mealtime. "I second that."

Another frown from Elsie. "I'm not sure. I've never dealt with something like this before. At the very least you'll have to try not to share with one another if you can help it. It'll only make it work."

"But we'll have to share if we want to catch-" Rift elbowed me in the side and I snapped my mouth shut. Usually there wasn't anything to keep me from telling Elsie about my cases, but with the federal government involved, that might not be the case. "Nevermind. Anyway, wouldn't it be better if we could figure out how to reverse it?"

"Actually, I have a theory about that. If you keep using magic like you normally would, you'll probably use up the foreign magic in your system first. Then it'll be back to normal."

"And with the spell already in place, we only have to wait for it to alert us to his location. So we've got magic to burn."

"Then what? Just burn up magic until we knock ourselves out? Literally?"

"Yes," Elsie said simply. I grinned widely.

"Then I've got an idea."

Chapter Four

"And where do you think you're going?"

I turned to face Cara, buttoning my jacket. "You heard Elsie. We're fine. So we're going out."

"Where are we going?" Rift asked curiously. He had retrieved his own jacket and was shrugging it on. His expression was curious, his body angled toward me while still aware of his handler.

"I'll tell you on the way." I grabbed my keyring and headed for the door, not giving Cara a chance to protest. With a mostly clean bill of health from Elise and the only alternative waiting around the apartment for the spell to indicate something, I needed get out of the apartment. The fact that I got to spend a little time with Rift, a sorcerer around my own age, was an added bonus. Most sorcerers our age attended special schools, at least the ones who could afford the gold-lined price tag. Those who couldn't made do with summer camps, weekend workshops, or covert meeting with more experienced magic users, which often got them in over their head. Kids like us had to deal with our magic any way we could, often without any help from friends or family, who simply couldn't deal with what they couldn't understand. My father had never been in the picture, and was no doubt ashamed of the fact that he had a sorceress for a daughter. He was the son of an influential senator, destined for greatness himself. My mother had been an ambitious college student, following him in order to research the effects that politics had on a person's outlook on life. Their tryst had been brief and eventful, but he had married his perfect woman right after, the beautiful heir to an oil fortune. When my mother had discovered that she was pregnant and had tried to tell him, she had never even gotten close. I had never spoken to my father, nor been any closer to him than a TV screen. As far as I was concerned, it could stay that way.

My mother and the rest of my family had dealt with my powers as best as I could, and I loved them for it. Unfortunately, I had made some bad choices, and they had led me down a dark path. Fortunately, it had led me here, to my life now, and Rift. That he was attractive didn't hurt, nor did the fact that we had permission, and in fact doctor's orders, to use our magic. That was more than enough for me.

There was no point trying to hail a taxi in wall to wall traffic, so we walked quietly together, dodging other people speed walking to their destination. The traffic was at a virtual stop, but the people on the sidewalk were bustling. Vendors selling hot dogs, almost certainly fake designer purses, and various other wares caught Rift's attention. I considered stopping, but I was looking forward to blowing off some steam, especially if it meant that I could get some sleep tonight. Considering last night's incident, the thought of getting some sleep was only partly attractive, but I was smart enough to realize that I needed to rest if I, or we, were going to stand any chance at capturing a guy like Edgar Logan.

Within ten minutes I was pointing Rift down a short side street. There were a few small houses on one side, but the other side was completely dominated by a massive brick building. A large white sign was erected in the front yard, but none of the lettering was legible; crimson paint was splashed haphazardly over the the words. Rage flooded through me at the sight. Rift's eyes dropped to my balled fists as magic flared in the gaps between my knuckles and closed fingers. It must have been unspeakably odd for him, to see his magic on my fingertips. It was odd enough for me, to see blue in my hands instead of purple.

"Come on," I said tightly, leading him up the sidewalk. There was a screened, wrap around porch, one that I knew for a fact would be locked from the inside. I knocked on the door and a face appeared almost instantly. The older woman's face split in a grin. Her white teeth flashed in her face. Magic users either aged very well, by turning their magic inwards to erase the signs of their age, or very poorly, because of all of the energy and power we expended over the course of our lifetime. She was somewhere in between. Her hair was a soft, shiny silver, trimmed neatly and dangling halfway between her chin and her collarbones. She was a good friend of mine, and it was good to see her again; I hadn't been able to come here as often as I would have liked lately. She didn't seem to mind, but I did.

"Scandal! Come in." There was a soft click as the deadbolt drew back; I stepped back as the door creaked open, forcing Rift to retreat as well. "And who is your friend?"

"Mabel, this is Rift. Rift, this is the leader of Magical Mercy House, Mabel." Rift nodded politely as she led us into the house. Several patients were laid up in the downstairs rooms, pale casts encasing their limbs. To the left was a short hallway that led to the kitchen, with a short table below a mirror. The table was completely empty but for an open binder. All visitors had to sign in there, but Mabel ignored it. She led us instead to the right and up a curving staircase. There were rooms splattered off of each landing, but Mabel led us to the the very top. This was where all the sickest people were housed, far away from the hustle and bustle of the main floor. Their sickness wasn't necessarily fatal; they needed only to wait for a powerful sorcerer to heal them. That was the whole purpose of Magical Mercy House. People came here to be cared for, to be healed with magic; they paid well for the opportunity. The broken down appearance of the property, the long, if green, grass, and the vandalized sign, were because of protesters and the hate that they felt toward this place. There were some that believed only medicine could heal people, not magic. Those people made their displeasure known often. We were just lucky that there hadn't been a violent protest out front like there had been the last few times I'd come. Sometimes the protests were non violent, taking up a post across the street, chanting and hoisting homemade signs. They occasionally hassled patients coming in, but it didn't happen as often as it could have. The fact that there were sorcerers inside that were very capable of turning them into a mushroom put a damper on all but the meanest of spirits.

"So we're healing people," Rift said, realization dawning. He nodded, running his fingers through his hair once more, brushing it back from his lean face. "That is a good use of power, I will admit that."

"I thought so." He grinned back. His long fingers were

scratching at the pocket of his jeans, my magic flickering on his fingertips, violet against the blue of the denim. It was a sign of nervous energy that I was used to seeing, because I did it quite a bit. The lack of sleep was starting to hit me, even with the excess magic in my veins, I was yawning. The energy from the magic was warring with the lack of sleep, with the end result being that I felt strung out and snappy.

"See you later," Rift said easily, following Mabel into another room. I headed to the next door and knocked, entering only after there was a feeble invitation to enter from within. There was a simple chair with floral seat and back cushions shoved into the corner, angled toward the bed. The woman in the bed put her book down on her lap and closed it, smiling in greeting. The bushy red tassel jutting from the bookmark within bumped against the woman's leg as she thumped the book nervously on her thigh. A partially dressed, very buxom woman swooned in a beefy man's arms. I fought not to roll my eyes, but I wasn't judging. I was more of a fantasy or historical fiction kind of girl, with the occasional science fiction or contemporary romance thrown in. If she wanted to spend her time laid up in bed reading a bodice ripper, more power to her. I wasn't one to judge someone by their reading choices.

The woman laid the book on the bedside table and folded her hands primly over her stomach. Her long nails were painted a soft coral, tiny splashes of color against the blue and white checkers of the hand made quilt. Mabel made these quilts herself, and everyone here knew their value. The woman in the bed fiddled nervously with the edge, watching my face and waiting to hear what I had to say. I didn't keep her in suspense for long.

"I'm Scandal. I'm here to see what I can do for you."

I seated myself in the chair, lifting it carefully in order to pull it closer to the side of the bed; Mabel would have my head if I scratched her nice wooden floors, but I wanted to be comfortable while I was in a healing trance. The woman's hands were cool as I took them in my own, willing my magic to rise to the surface.

The excess magic from Rift was overflowing my "well" of magic, centered behind my collarbones. It leapt eagerly at my call, warm light winding around my forearms like an affectionate corn snake before reaching my hands. Once more I startled by the brilliant blue hue, although the young woman, no more than five years my senior, noticed nothing amiss. She wouldn't have, since she had never worked with me before. In point of fact, I had never laid eyes on her before in my life. While I knew the color of the magic in my grasp was odd and out of the ordinary, she knew nothing of the sort. I kept my face impassive so that the patient couldn't sense my unease. With her sickness, she was scared enough already without realizing that the sorceress pumping magic into her body wasn't playing at the top of her game. I closed my eyes and eased into my magic, centering myself before easing it through my hands and into hers.

Almost immediately I could see what was wrong. I could see the faint shadow of what should have been, overpowered by a dark shadow that slithered from vein to vein, weakening her. This was a magical virus, one created by a sorcerer to weaken his enemies. Some sorcerers did it for money, others merely for fun, making me wonder which category this poor woman fit into. Not that it really mattered. Either way, she was still very sick. Magic had made her ill, and magic was the only thing that could make her healthy again.

I eased magic into the darkness and pushed magic

through the gaps. Slowly and with great effort, I was able to purge it from her body, popping the spots of darkness like soap bubbles. By the time I was finished, there was no shadow to eclipse the brilliant light of a healthy body.

My eyes were barely open when the woman lunged forward and hugged me. I grunted as her full weight landed on my shoulders and torso, since she was hanging half in and half out of the bed. I braced my hand on the bed and helped ease her back, my weak muscles protesting. I smiled and nodded as she spoke.

"Thank you so much," she enthused. I nodded and backed out of the room, closing the door behind me and leaning against the wall. Rift was against the opposite wall, his head leaned back and eyes closed. I did the same, reaching down to take stock of my magic. There was still plenty of it left to keep healing, and Rift's magic was still there as well, although depleted.

"I didn't realize how much of a rush that would be." Rift sounded both impressed and incensed by the discovery, but I was just impressed. By him, to be more exact. It had taken me years and lots of practice to be as good at healing as I was, and I still couldn't do anything delicate. I could purge systems of maladies and mend small injuries, like cuts or scrapes, but healing intricate things like bones or torn ligaments was far beyond the reach of my skills. As far as I knew, Rift had no training in healing whatsoever. I shouldn't have been surprised that he was so good at it, but I kind of was.

Most sorcerers had a specialty, a task that they were trained for. Necromancers, Spirit Speakers, Heart Singers, Healers. Rift and I were more like general practitioners, those who possessed magic but not an innate affinity for any one type of use. We could work nearly any type of magic, although not with as much skill as someone who spent their entire lives studying one particular area of magic. It was like expecting a heart surgeon to be able to fix your kitchen sink. They might have some basic knowledge of how it worked, but they wouldn't be able to repair it as well as a plumber. It was the same way with Rift and I.

I chuckled briefly in response to his statement. "I did. I come here every Friday night to burn off power. I only do it at the end of the week because I don't have to work the next day." I smiled wryly. "Otherwise I wouldn't be able to sleep."

"Bet you would have liked to come here last night. Looks like it was a sleepless night."

I put my hand to my face self-consciously. I'd noticed the dark purple circles under my eyes this morning with a glance in the mirror, but I hadn't had time to put makeup on to cover it up, and I had foolishly thought that no one would look closely enough to notice. Apparently I had been wrong.

"Is it really that obvious?"

His full lips made a silent O of horror as he realized what I thought. "No! Of course not," he said quickly. "That's not what I meant. I've just had enough of them to recognize the signs." He motioned to his own face, presumably at the dark shadows, but I was snared by his dark green eyes. They were dark with power; I was sure that mine were the same.

"I have the opposite problem," he confided. Without thinking about it, we had both shifted on our respective walls, so that we were no longer angled toward each other but were now directly across, our long legs nearly touching. Rift was smiling softly, not quite making eye contact but still looking at my face.

"What do you mean?"

"I don't have enough power. I can control what I have, but there isn't enough to do anything big."

"And I have far too much, but control is," I made a face, "sometimes a challenge. Aren't we a pair."

My phone buzzed and I dug it out of my pocket. Of course, it was from Cara.

You guys okay? We're starting to get concerned.

I sent back, *We're fine. Be home in a little bit.*

"Everything alright?" Rift asked softly. He had created a tiny horse in his palm while I was looking away, a soft violet creature that pranced in his palm, directly on his life line.

"Everything is fine." I crossed the hall to join him. He rocked back on his heels like he wanted to back away, the tiny equine flickering, then solidifying when I raised my palm to line up with his. Modeling mine after his, a blue mare joined the purple. An extra push of magic allowed her to move on her own, with no help from me. To my surprise, she stepped from my palm to his and touched noses with the other of her species. I glanced at Rift in surprise, then quickly down at the horses as mine flickered from blue to purple, and his did the reverse. They shimmered out of existence, the magic powering them cut off.

I cleared my throat. "We should go." With the last of Rift's magic purged from my system, the side effects I had been expecting earlier had arrived in full force. Rift was in the same boat; he was leaning against the wall, his knees flexing as he slid down. My knees didn't flex, but rather gave away entirely, and I hit the floor hard.

Chapter Five

This time it wasn't a pinch that woke me, but rather soft voices. I lay there for a few minutes with my eyes closed, listening to the conversation.

"I told her that it was a bad idea. I knew I should have gone with her. I shouldn't have let her go with some kid we barely know."

"I'm sitting right here, you know," a voice said peevishly. From the answer, it should have been Rift, but the voice was too deep to be his. Probably Elliott.

I opened my eyes and sat up against the hard headboard, wincing. I was shaking, despite the fact that Cara had put my jacket on while I was asleep. I was in a bed in what was unmistakably at Magical Mercy House. The woman I'd healed earlier was in the chair I had been sitting in, grinning wryly at our reversed positions. Cara and Elliott were standing, their arms crossed as they glared at one another. Even Mabel was there, seated on the edge of the bed. The only one missing was Rift, which I commented on.

"Where's Rift?" I asked.

Elliott jerked his chin toward the far wall. "Knocked out in the next room. Now that one of you is awake, we can go home." I bit down the urge the urge to point out that it was *my* home, since my modest apartment had somehow become our base of operations. With that, Elliott left the room. Mabel and the young woman I had healed followed him out; as soon as they were gone, Cara locked the door and tossed a black duffel bag onto the foot of the bed. I reluctantly lowered the covers to unzip it, then shed my jean jacket. Inside were long johns, fuzzy socks, a pair of soft boots that were almost like slippers, and a thick sweatshirt. Cara turned her back to give me some privacy.

"If I hear a thud and you've passed out, I'm leaving you there this time," she grumbled. I rolled my eyes; clearly she was still upset that Rift and I had ignored her advice to stay at home and now she wanted to be sure that I felt her displeasure, which I did, although I didn't regret our choice. I dressed as quickly as I could with my shaking hands, then pulled on a pair of fingerless gloves stuffed in the pockets of the sweatshirt, wincing as I did so. Large works of magic singed my fingertips, like I'd done to my bed sheets last night. Already tender from the impartial working on the roof this morning, this last bit of magic had crossed the line from tender to fully burned. They would heal in a few days, but in the meantime, I had some salve at home that would speed up the process.

Cara turned back around once I stopped rustling around, zipping her jacket smoothly as she turned. She helped me to my feet and out the door. Elliott was in front of us, Rift slung over his shoulder. There was a dark unmarked car waiting outside; Elliott placed Rift in the back, none too gently, and climbed into the driver's seat. Cara deposited me into the backseat, next to Rift. I scooted over, buttoning my jacket over the top of my sweatshirt, my weak arms wrestling with where the hood was tucked under the denim. With almost no magic to speak of, I felt like a dried out husk. Rift was sprawled across the backseat, his long hair spilling across his face.

"Shouldn't we buckle him in or something?" I asked doubtfully, fastening my own seatbelt as I spoke. He looked so innocent laying there, I hated to wake him, but I also didn't want him to die because of midtown traffic. Not that I could have woken him anyway; I could hardly tell that he was breathing.

Up front, Elliott snorted. He was doing his best to nudge the car into traffic, but it was no good; there was a solid wall of metal that even he couldn't slide into.

"After the stunt you two pulled, he's lucky I didn't put him in the trunk. He and I are going to have words when he finally wakes up."

Alrighty then, I mouthed to myself. I was afraid I would wake him if I tried to push him upright in order to buckle him in; I compromised by unbuckling my belt, scooting into the middle, and pulling his head gently into my lap.

There was a nagging sense of something odd within my magic, but without more of it, it was a struggle to find the issue. I leaned forward, balancing my left hand on the back of Elliott's seat. We were still kinked diagonally, trying to slither into traffic, so I wasn't overly worried about distracting the driver.

"So what was that earlier, when you shut the chief down? What did you stop him from telling us?"

Cara dug around in the bag at her feet. With a crinkle of paper, she withdrew a piece of paper and twisted to pass it over the top of the seat to me. It was a photocopy of what seemed to be a letter. My eyes skimmed quickly over the small, neat handwriting and widened when I saw the signature at the bottom.

Forever yours,

Edgar Logan

"Oh, geez," I mumbled, returning to the beginning of the letter with fresh eyes and renewed interest.

To whom it may concern,

I have been informed by reliable sources that you and your team are searching for me. Your team consists of Elliott Roth, Cara Kane, Rift Hartkin, and Scandal Becker. I understand that you are only working to accomplish the task set before you. However, I must protest, and offer an ultimatum. If you leave me to continue my dealings in peace, none of you shall be harmed and you shall be richly rewarded. If you continue to interfere, I will be forced to place a bounty on each of your heads. Furthermore, I will use an artifact in my posession to create a massive storm, one that may very well destroy the city. If it does, it will be on your heads.

Forever yours,

Edgar Logan

"That's alarming," I pointed out, which was rather obvious but still needed to be said. "I see now why you stopped the chief from telling us. So what are we going to do?"

Elliott gunned the car into traffic, throwing me back into the seat. Rift was starting to rouse, shifting and murmuring in his sleep. Elliott ignored his charge, snaking into the nearest alley, speeding down the smaller, less congested side streets. This wasn't the way back to my apartment, which meant that we were heading back to the station. Not that it mattered, because both Rift and I were tapped dry in the magic department.

Cara twisted around in her seat and snatched the letter back, clearly still upset about the day's escapades.

"We're going to the station," she said shortly, like I wasn't smart enough to have figured that out already. Clearly she wasn't happy that I hadn't followed her advice, although it shouldn't have surprised her, since it wasn't the first time. I wasn't exactly happy that I hadn't listened either, but this wasn't exactly a typical situation. At the time, following Elsie's directive had seemed like the best idea, and going to Magical Mercy had been the best option. That way, at least we were doing something useful while we were burning off our magic, not just sitting on the living room floor creating pretty lights until we literally knocked ourselves out. Now, with only a trickle of magic at my disposal, an unconscious teammate, two peeved adults, and a bounty on all our heads, there was more than enough to worry about without dredging up the past.

"There's another letter waiting. The chief says that it's a warning that we're now hunted."

I winced and reached once more for my magic. There was a little more now, but I still felt weak and shaky. I had a nagging sense that something else was wrong. I carefully propped Rift up and twisted around in my seat. The same silver car had been tailing us for the past few streets, no mean feat considering how fast Elliott was driving on the narrow lanes. They were one or two car lengths behind, but they were never out of sight. Now that I knew to look for it, I half turned back to the front so as not to be so obvious, watching from the corner of my eye.

"Elliott, we're being tailed," I said as nonchalantly as I

could muster. His eyes flicked to the rearview mirror and to the silver car I had indicated. He slowed down and turned onto a street that was closed for construction. The silver car cruised to a stop behind us.

Wonder of wonders, Rift chose that moment to wake up. He groaned and sat up, rubbing his forehead.

"What's happening?"

"A magical arms dealer put a bounty on our heads, we're being tailed, and Elliott here decided the most logical thing to do was to pull into an abandoned site, filled with dangerous objects and places to hide a dead body, in order to confront them." I took a deep breath at the conclusion of my tirade. "Oh, and neither you nor I has any magic left to defend ourselves with, since we've completely wiped ourselves out. Am I missing anything?"

Elliott had shut off the car and was keeping a close eye on the car behind us, its lights blinding when I turned to look. Two soft clicks as Elliott and Cara checked their guns.

"You're with two law enforcement agents. You're as safe as we can make you. For once, do as you're told, and just stay in the car."

"But-" Rift protested; slamming car doors punctuated the end of the statement. He huffed and we both twisted to watch the confrontation, knees brushing. I squinted, my forearm braced on the back of the seat, trying to see better. More slamming doors. As Rift and I watched in horror, five armed men forced our partners to their knees. I had only a moment to recognize that the click I heard behind me was the door opening before a strong pair of hands dragged me out of the car.

"Let go!" I threw an elbow backwards, but another lug had joined the party, dragging my wrists out in front of me and slapping shackles on them, like old fashioned manacles. As a wave of weakness washed over me, I knew what they were. These cuffs were spelled to lock down magic. Even now I could see the marks carved into the metal, like runes on the cover of a fantasy novel. The fact that I was tapped for magic no longer mattered, since I couldn't even feel it, let alone use it.

Rift and I struggled, but the goon squad shoved us into the trunk of the silver car before we knew it. Apparently the bounty on our heads was in full effect, and these guys had come to collect.

Chapter Six

"I know you said you were going to throw me in the trunk, but this is ridiculous," Rift said with false cheerfulness. Elliott rolled his eyes. We were all bound to chairs in a dimly lit warehouse. Cara and Elliott wore plain handcuffs, while we sorcerers were adorned with the same shackles as before, as well as spelled iron chains tight around our chests and ankles. All in all, it was an unpleasant arrangement, not lessened by the fact that I still had pins and needles from being shoved into the trunk with Rift. The adults had been allowed to ride in the backseat, for whatever reason, but we'd been in the boot. If I'd thought sharing my apartment was awkward, it was nothing compared to the agony of being crammed into a car trunk with another person, practically on top of each other every time we hit a bump.

Cara sat up, perking up like a hunting dog on point. A hand clamped onto my shoulder and I writhed away, chains rattling. The man who stood before us was broad shouldered and athletic, with slicked back gray hair. There was a thin line around his neck, in the shape of a thick chain.

"You two don't look much like sorcerers to me," he said doubtfully, looking us up and down appraisingly. I had to admit, two pale, shivering teenagers in sweatshirts in jeans may not have fallen in line with the common idea of magic users.

Rift arched one eyebrow. His chin was tilted up in challenge. "Were you expecting robes and a magic wand?" he snarked. The man pulled up a chair, angling so that he was leaning toward us but could still see the others.

After a moment of tense silence, the man chuckled. His goons, who had taken up positions in a loose circle around us, laughed too. It was the kind of half hearted, forced laughter that signified someone not sure how much they were willing to commit to something.

"Not sure what I was expecting. My sorcerers look a little more worldly is all." He jerked his head toward a man and a woman in the corner with magic on their fingers, silky yellow and burnt orange respectively. The man wore faded jeans and a grimy gray t-shirt, with a large silver hoop in his left ear. The woman wore all black, ripped skinny jeans and a tank top with studded combat boots. A chain wound around her narrow waist served as a belt. The man seemed disinterested, but the woman was making determined, rather aggressive eye contact with me. I vacillated between glaring back and looking away, then decided to look away. Challenging her like that was not smart, especially considering that I wasn't very experienced with combat spells even under the best of circumstances. Being chained to a chair with magic proof chains and no magic anyway was by no means that time.

"Perhaps your 'more worldly' sorcerers feel a little threatened by us," Rift said coolly. "Judging by the lady's glare." So he'd noticed too. The two came toward us, the male sorcerer stepping behind the leader's chair but the woman standing firmly in front of us. Burnt orange sparks swirled around her sharp nails, filed to a point like a letter opener. I refused to look away this time, even as she leaned close to my face, close enough that my own magic would have been uneasy if I had been able to sense its presence. I wanted to lean away, but I couldn't.

"That's where you're wrong. I'm not threatened, just curious as to how whelps like you merit a bounty from the biggest arms dealer on the magical circuit."

I squinted at the leader. The other two sorcerers were standing, which may have been a sign of deference, or it may have been something more. The way he was sitting, shoulders hunched and stomach pulled toward his spine, made me think that he was in some kind of pain. The other two, and even the goons, all wore charms to prevent magical tampering, but the leader didn't. It was possible that he thought he was too tough for it. Or, if my hunch was right, it was because it was too late to prevent tampering.

"I'd like to know that as well, but we're not being paid to ask questions." The leader stood, limping toward the door. "And once I call them, you won't have to worry about it much longer."

"Wait!" I blurted. "If I can break your curse, will you let us go?" My three compatriots stared at me, startled, but not nearly as much so as the mob boss.

"I don't know what you're talking about." Even though I wasn't an actual detective, not in terms of the badge, the salary, or the respect, I had still been working with the police for long enough to recognize a lie when I saw one. It wasn't even a very good try.

"Take these chains off and I'll lift whatever curse has been placed on you. I do that, you let us all go, and act like you never saw us."

I could see the indecision flickering in his brown eyes. The war between the money he could make and living an uncursed life was eating him up inside. Between one blink and the next, the decision was made. He snapped his meaty fingers.

"Untie her. Now," he ordered. The woman began to protest, but the man was already moving, unwinding the chains around my torso and wrists. As soon as they were off, the feeling rushed back into my limbs, as well as my magic. Between when we'd been tossed in the trunk of a car and now, when the chains were taken off, a pool of purple power had regenerated. I could only hope it would be enough for the task at hand.

"I might need him too," I said cautiously, keeping my face as smooth and innocent as possible. Rift did the same, lowering his chin and adopting a submissive posture. None of them were dumb enough to buy that act.

The mob boss snorted. "Nice try. If you can't do it alone, then you're worth more to me gone."

I shrugged apologetically at Rift and followed the boss and his sorcerers to another room. Once again, the big man sat immediately. Since no one had offered me a chair, nor did it seem like they were going to in the foreseeable future, I sat on the floor and crossed my legs, trying to ignore the threatening presences around me as I closed my eyes to concentrate. I felt around for the curse, but first I had to set it apart from the orange and yellow magic woven around it, like a basket. Or a cage. It looked like the two sorcerers had tried to stop, or at least slow, the curse. Although largely unsuccessful, that interference was almost certainly the reason that he was still alive.

It took a few minutes and a fistful of power for me to untangle the spells around the larger curse. I pushed power and tugged on it, dismantling as carefully as I could. Some spells were known to attack a sorcerer as they were being removed, latching onto any source of magic and infecting it. From what I could tell of the working, a woman had placed it there, with the intention of slowly crippling the mob boss. Whoever she was, she was inexperienced with casting spells; there were several openings for me to exploit as I ripped it apart.

I blinked my eyes open and shifted, neck cracking stiffly. "I'm finished. Feel any different?"

The woman crouched, her lips moving as she spoke to the mob boss. He was rubbing his knees, then the back of his neck. I couldn't hear much, but I did catch what I thought might be a name: Razor.

"Are you Razor?" I guessed. All three shot me surprised looks, but the oldest man nodded. He helped me to my feet, holding most of my weight since I was weak from the magic consumption.

"I'm Razor. Thank you for lifting my curse."

I nodded in acknowledgement. "I'm glad to be of help, especially if it means you'll let us go." I watched him carefully for signs that he meant to back out of our deal, gathering a fistful of magic but keeping it coiled just beneath the surface of my skin so that neither of the other mages were aware that I was rallying what little power I had on hand.

Razor chuckled and dropped one paw onto my shoulder. "A deal is a deal. My sorcerers, good as they are, couldn't do any more than slow it down. It's been eating me up for years, piece by piece. I'm just grateful that you could help."

We headed into the next room and unbound my friends. Rift jumped up immediately, magic flickering on his fingertips; clearly he wasn't trying very hard to hide his magic. As I'd feared, the woman responded, and the other man followed her lead. Soon all four of us had magic on our fingertips, squaring off with our charges at our backs. I held my hands up, one on Rift's chest to hold him back and the other extended toward our enemies.

"Whoa! We're all friends here. There's no need for this to get ugly," I soothed.

I intentionally let go of my magic, trying to show a sign of good faith that I didn't want to hurt them. The woman's sparks dropped soon after mine, with Rift's last. As soon as the mob boss re entered the room, she wrapped her arm around his waist, and I couldn't help smirking at the fact that my suspicions had been correct. The woman's long brown hair swayed as she smiled at Razor, then turned the soft smile on us. She offered me a hand wreathed in burnt orange to shake, but this time, it wasn't a threat. It was a peace offering.

Just as it had with Rift, the handshake with both of our magic active allowed us to get to know one another better, and reach a sort of agreement. We weren't as different as I had thought, so it was easy to find common ground to stand on. Her grin widened.

"I'm Esther. Thank you for helping my husband." My eyes widened as she grasped my forearm and pulled me into a tight hug, which I returned. She wasn't exactly what she looked like, but then again, who was? "It was killing me that I couldn't save him. We tried our best, but…"

"I understand," I said softly. The introductions continued with Cara and Elliott, rubbing their sore wrists ruefully but seeming none the worse for wear otherwise. Esther left the group halfway through; Razor didn't so much turn to watch her go as follow her with his eyes, his expression soft and fond. It was odd to see such a gentle emotion on his tough, swarthy face, but I was glad of it, for multiple reasons. By the time the introductions were through, Esther was back with sandwiches and snacks. My rumbling stomach thanked her, and she laughed softly.

"I know I'm hungry. It only makes sense that the curse-breaker would be too," she grinned. We both chose one of the small sandwiches from the tray, cut neatly into precise triangles, and touched the edges as if we were toasting with a glass of fine champagne. Cobalt didn't so much as select a sandwich as scoop up a handful and shove them into his mouth; we rolled our eyes.

I took a meditative bite of the tiny sandwich, surprised to find that it was turkey and provolone cheese. I was normally more of a ham and cheddar girl myself, but I didn't mind it. "Cursebreaker," I mused. "I kind of like that."

Rift snorted into his bottle of water, pausing in the middle of washing his mouth out. "What, Scandal isn't enough for you?"

I fought not to wince, even as that evinced a chuckle from everyone else. The origin of my name was rather a sore spot, one that I didn't really want to get into with all of these virtual strangers. Even Cara had only a hazy idea, and I wasn't sure that I was ready to share with Rift yet. The fact that I'd been chained to a chair ten minutes ago and in the trunk of a car ten minutes before that reminded me that there were other things to worry about.

"Now then. Tell us everything you know about Edgar Logan."

Esther shrugged loosely, still chewing on her sandwich. She was perched on the edge of the table, with Razor's hand massaging her hand. "There's honestly not much to tell."

Chapter Seven

"Logan is offering a hundred thousand dollars for each of them, delivered to him alive. A twenty five thousand dollar bonus if it's within the next two days."

"Why does he need us alive?" I wondered aloud. It had been bothering me since Razor and Esther had first told us their story and it was still bothering me now, back at the station. "Don't get me wrong, I'm glad that there aren't standing orders to kill us on sight, but why? What does he want from us?"

Razor shrugged, but Esther was picking at the studded cuffs on her wrist. I leaned forward so that I was in her line of sight. "Esther, what aren't you telling us?"

She looked first at Rift, who was fooling with his bracelet as well. While they had been on the outs at first, once we had all gotten over our attitudes, those two had connected. The man from earlier was seated farther down the table. Rift and I sat across from Razor and Esther; Cara and Elliott were standing with the chief.

"I have an idea why he wants you alive," Esther admitted grudgingly. "To do what he threatened to do to me."

Razor paled, which was a drastic change to his ruddy complexion. The tan line on his neck that I had noticed before was from an amulet to ward off magical interference, which he'd taken off while he'd been cursed, claiming that it had seemed kind of redundant; he had replaced it as soon as the curse was lifted. "What are you talking about?"

Esther laced her fingers through his. "When we first heard about Logan coming to the city, word was already out that he wanted to have a meeting with the sorcerers, so I went. He told us all, in no uncertain terms, what he would do to us if we didn't cooperate with him." She stopped to take a breath and the other sorcerer, Edge, took over seamlessly.

"Edgar Logan is a madman with access to dangerous artifacts. He can't use magic himself, but he desperately wants to. He has an artifact that will strip a sorcerer of their powers."

Rift was white as powdered sugar. "So that's what he wants with us."

Edge nodded. "Edgar Logan is very much a 'waste not, want not' kind of man. Why would he have you killed when he can steal your power and *then* have you killed? It would be a waste."

Cara raised her hand. "Why us, though?" she motioned between herself and Elliott, who nodded in agreement. "We don't have any magic, so there should be no reason for him to want us alive."

That elicited a shrug. "Who knows? Maybe he just wanted the full set, maybe he wanted you guys as leverage, maybe he hates cops. I can only explain so much of a lunatic's reasoning."

Chief looked up from his notes. "And you said that Logan's messengers brought you the chains and everything you needed to hold my sorcerers captive, is that correct?"

"Yeah, why?"

I could see Chief cringe at the informality of the response, but he pulled it together and lifted one of the chains carefully, holding it with the tip of a pencil like he didn't want to touch it. Or maybe he didn't want to contaminate evidence. "Because I recognize this. There's a seedy little man at the outskirts of the city that makes plenty of things like this. They've given my sorcerers a lot of trouble over the years."

Cara was already pulling on her jacket. "We'll go check it out." I grabbed a granola bar from the table and shoved it into my jacket pocket as I stood. Rift stumbled over his chair in his haste to reach the door, but Chief was already there, barring the way with his arms crossed.

"And where do you think you're going?"

I motioned, thinking it should be fairly obvious. "Out. To follow the lead."

"No. Your handlers can go, because they can handle themselves, but you two are going home." I crossed my arms and arched an eyebrow; Cara sighed audibly behind me. "Because they handled themselves so much better than we did today," I snarked. Rift snorted softly.

"I noticed you were the ones in the trunk." That was Elliott. I rounded on him and Rift stiffened, like he wasn't sure whose side he was on. "Yeah, but apparently we can't handle ourselves," I said sarcastically. "You're so much more in control when you're handcuffed in the back seat."

"Enough!" Chief barked. "My mind is made up. Uniforms will escort you back to your apartment, where you will stay until further notice. Understood?"

"Fine," I seethed. He looked suspicious at how easily I had acquiesced, and he had reason to be. Cara was taking no chances.

"Come here." I turned to face her with a sigh. With a speed born of doing this very thing to suspects, she slapped one cuff onto my wrist and the other onto Rift's. I raised my wrist and stared at her in minute shock, dragging Rift's with it. He made a 'what gives?' motion and glared at Elliott, who snorted.

"Don't look at me. I think she's got the right idea. I know you too well to think that you'll let this go."

Rift put his free hand over his heart, wounded. "I am hurt. I can't believe that you think we would disobey a direct order."

"The lack of faith in us is astounding," I agreed. Snorts from the adults, but the chief stepped aside to let us and the uniform head out. We had a bit of difficulty when we both tried to step through at the same time, then stepped back. Rift motioned and I went first, my cuffed wrist twisted painfully behind my back. We couldn't walk more than about a foot apart without being pulled back together, and we bounced off each other a few times before we managed to get the distance right so that we could walk side by side at a somewhat respectable distance. The uniformed officer led us to an undercover vehicle in the garage. By habit I swerved toward Cara's car, tangling us up; Rift tugged me back into place, smiling slightly.

It was a short drive back to my apartment, now that the

traffic had subsided. The uniform walked us up and saw us inside; only then did he produce the key to the cuffs and set us free. I rubbed my wrist, then reached to flick the light switch, illuminating the darkness.

"Thank you," I told the uniform. I was majorly ticked off that I'd been left behind yet again, but it wasn't fair to take that out on him. I was sure that he didn't want to be stuck with two moody, peeved teenagers anymore than we wanted to be escorted by him. He nodded respectfully and turned away, leaving me to close the door behind him.

"Hungry?" I asked, my voice a few decibels louder than normal. Rift raised a brow questioningly and I nodded at the door. The cop was still outside the door, no doubt to make sure we were actually going to stay put before he left. Poor guy, thinking we weren't smart enough to wait until after he was gone to make our move. The question was asked purely for his benefit; Rift's eyes lit as he caught on.

"I could use something. Granola bars can only go so far."

As we spoke, I rattled a few bowls and opened the refrigerator door, all the sounds of a meal being made. The tendril of magic I had extended into the hallway as a watchdog receded as the officer headed down the stairwell. I waited a few minutes, then opened a window and slithered on onto the fire escape. Rift's face appeared in the window, and he spoke as he slipped out.

"So do you have a car hidden somewhere, or…?"

I shook my head, taking the iron stairs two at a time. They felt rickety, but I knew for a fact that they were safe. Once a month, I magically reinforced all of the fire escapes on the surrounding buildings, and made sure that all of the fire preventative equipment was up to date. There was absolutely no way that someone was going to get hurt because of faulty equipment.

Rift seemed to have his reservations; he wasn't quite pelting down the stairs like I was, but he was keeping up.

"Nope. No car. Cara usually drives me, but since that isn't really an option, I'm going to call a taxi." I whistled; by the time we reached the curb, a checkered cab was already waiting. Rift opened the door for me and piled in. I recited the address I had snuck from the report, then added "As quickly as you can, please."

"You know we're not going to beat them there," Rift stated. I nodded.

"I don't care who made the shackles. I care about who bought them. No doubt it was a middle man, but if we can find the middle man, we might be able to trace it back to Logan."

Rift reached into the messenger bag wedged between his feet and withdrew a file folder.

"I might have an idea about that. See this?" I opened the folder and he leaned over to point, one hand braced on the seat between us for balance. He was so close that I could smell his breath, which smelled like peanut butter from the granola bar we had shared. I tried to ignore it.

He pointed to a piece of paper torn from a small notebook, filled partially with tiny writing and clipped to a police sketch.

"This is a description we found a few months ago of one of Logan's accomplices. It fits with the description that Razor and Esther gave of the woman who brought them the chains. I think she's the one we need to find."

I flipped back the page to look at the sketch. It showed

an older woman with colored-in silver hair and high cheek-bones with dark, haunted eyes. It was the face of a woman who had struggled all her life. I felt a glimmer of pity for her, quashed only by the fact that she was helping a man who had put a bounty on our heads. "Let's find her then."

Chapter Eight

"Crap," Rift and I chorused. Cara's unmarked car was parked outside a dingy building with no sign. If I squinted, I could see symbols painted on the building, almost entirely eclipsed by dirt and soot. The spells were to prevent entrance by anyone who meant harm to the owner; judging by their appearance, those sigils had been sorely tested before now. They weren't a problem for us, since we weren't looking to do him any harm. Just for information.

Rift paid for the taxi before I could, and we climbed out. I'd offered to pay, but he wouldn't take no for an answer, and it wasn't worth fighting about right now. We headed inside; a bell jangled as we stepped over the threshold.

Cara and Elliott, standing by the bar, turned to look as we entered. Their faces darkened. The man across the counter cleared his throat uncomfortably.

"Are you all together? All want the same thing?"

I'm going to kill you, Cara mouthed. I shrugged slightly, trying to convey that I was sorry that I had disobeyed her, but that there was a good reason for it.

Rift reached into his bag, dug around for a moment, and produced the sketch.

"Actually, we're looking for this woman." He slid the drawing across the countertop. The man barely spared it a glance.

"Sorry. I can't help you."

"I think you can," Rift pressed. "We have reason to believe that you've had dealings with this woman."

The man's small, dark eyes shifted away. I leaned on the counter, purple sparks flickering on my fingers and shimmering in my irises. His eyes widened, and the dim fluorescent lights glinted off the crown of his bald head as he stepped back.

"Two hours ago, I was chained up in a car trunk with one of *your* shackles," I jabbed one finger into the glass of the case; a pool of violet was gathering, spreading like spilled paint toward the little man. The slither was rather threatening, and entirely for show. It wasn't a threat to him; I wasn't feeding it any power. As I said, it was all for show. "You'll understand if I'm not inclined to be friendly toward you."

"Fine! I don't know her name, or where she lives."

"Then what do you know?" RIft asked doubtfully. His arms were crossed, his head tilted.

"When she'll be in next." He made a show of checking his watch, which was far too nice for him to be able to afford from legitimate dealings, but I tried to ignore it. Cara could deal with his shady deals later, after we were finished. "In less than an hour."

"Excuse us a moment," Cara said tightly. The four of us retreated to the rear of the store, out of earshot of the owner but where we could still keep a close eye on him in case he decided to try something fishy. I could tell from the flush in

Cara's high cheekbones that she wanted to yell at me, but she was right down to business.

"An hour's not a lot of time to set up a stakeout, but we can't risk losing our only lead to Logan. We'll have to do what we can in the time we have."

Elliott nodded in agreement. "As unhappy as I am with you two, you'll be useful. If we can't take her in ourselves, you can be the backup."

I nodded eagerly. Rift did as well. I hated disobeying Cara, but it seemed like that was all I had been doing lately. A tiny voice whispered that it was because of Rift, that I hadn't been nearly this rebellious before he came along, but I beat it down. My choices were my own. Yes, Rift was a part of those choices now, but I was still a functioning almost adult who had the final say. It wasn't fair to blame him when it was me that was at fault. I promised myself that I would make it up to Cara later.

Less than an hour later, we were all in place when the woman entered the store, the cheerful chime of the bell belying the seriousness of the situation. Her silver hair was medium length, partially obscuring a logo on the back of her faded jean jacket. She checked to see if there was anyone around, then slid a small bag across the counter. Cara and Elliott stepped out from the back room, guns drawn. The woman's eyes darted toward the door, but she didn't move.

"Come here," Elliott ordered. With his free hand he lifted his handcuffs from the back of his belt. He tossed them to her and she caught them with her left hand, barely moving.

"Put them on."

"No," she said flatly. In a flash she had grabbed the heavy bag and flung it at them. Glass shattered as one of the guns went off and a stray bullet caught one of the glass cases, the woman sprinting toward the door. I flung my hand out, throwing up a wall of purple shine. It was a tidal wave of violet and turquoise, mixed like an artist's palette; it seemed that Rift and I had had the same idea.

"Throwing things is rude," I said mildly. She reached into her back pocket and drew a switchblade, but other than flicking it open, she made no move to use it.

"Where is Edgar Logan?"

She chuckled darkly. Cara and Elliott were picking themselves up off the floor, their guns a few feet away on either side.

"I won't tell you." She held up a wagging finger as we protested. "I won't tell you, but I'll take you there."

Cara motioned with her gun. "Fine. Let's go."

She shook her head. "Not you two. I'll take the pups, and then we'll come back for you."

"Fine," I said immediately. Cara was already shaking her head, but I ignored her. "I'll go with you."

"Me too," Rift said. We were standing so closely that his chest brushed my back with each breath, a soft pant of exertion from holding the spell.

At the woman's direction, we handcuffed Cara and Elliott to one of the displays, despite their protests. The woman waited by the door, Elliott's gun cradled in her grip. Cara spoke in hushed tones as I tightened the cuffs.

"You know this is a terrible idea."

I held my hands out helplessly. "If you've got a better idea, I'm all ears. I'm well aware that this is both stupid and dangerous, but I don't see a better option." The cuff tightened and she winced. Rift helped me up from my crouch, squeezing my hand briefly as we headed for the door.

Once more we were in a car headed for the man that wanted to strip our powers and/or kill us. On the plus side, we weren't in the trunk this time. We were shackled again, wrist to wrist. They clinked gently as Rift held out his hand, palm up. I laced my fingers through his for comfort. Come what may, we were on our way.

Chapter Nine

"Get out." I stumbled as I was dragged out of the car, dragging Rift along. We were inside a warehouse; the garage door had rattled closed behind us. Wooden crates of all sizes filled the space, with tables here and there covered with papers. There were cages in the corner and what looked to be some sort of stone altar with iron chains in the center of the room, both of which filled me with a deep sense of unease. Rift glanced at me out of the corner of his eye and I shrugged.

The silver haired woman led us toward the altar, where a man was seated. His chin length black hair was salted with the same shade of silver. She went to join him in leaning against the stone, leaving us to stand awkwardly a few feet away. The man studied critically, jewelry flashing. All of it that I could see was spelled, for protection and non-interference. There was enough of it that it would have been making my hair stand on end if the shackles not been preventing me from accessing my gift.

"So. You two are the ones that have been causing me so much trouble. I expected you would be… older."

My expression didn't change. I'd had the same thought when I'd been brought on the case. However, the conclusion that I had reached was that they had been looking for power and control, not necessarily experience or age. Nevertheless, I was mildly insulted at the implication.

"I was expecting someone more like an old professor or a seedy arms dealer, and less like you're in a motorcycle gang." I paused. "I was right about the height though." Even the older woman was an inch or so taller than he, and I was a solid two inches taller than her. Rift snorted as the man's face tightened, coughing into his fist to hide his laughter.

"As I'm sure you know, my name is Edgar Logan. This is my mother, Edith." He gestured at the silver haired woman and I couldn't help widening my eyes. I'd thought that she was his errand runner, not his *mother*. I hadn't expected that at all.

I resisted the urge to cross my arms. My wrist was still chained to Rift's and doing that would make things a whole lot more awkward.

"You already know who we are," I pointed out peevishly. Actually, he probably knew a lot more than that. I shuddered to think what he had dug up about my past, maybe including the reason I had to work for the police.

"Yes, but I want to hear it from you."

"I'm Rift Hartkin."

"I'm Scandal Becker."

His eyes narrowed and he wagged a finger at me. "Ah ah. That's not your real name."

"It is my real name. Anything else is a falsehood. I'm not that girl. I never was."

"Why don't you tell your friend what your real name is? As a team building exercise, of course."

I swallowed. I desperately wanted to insist that that was my real name, the only name that anyone knew me by, but I knew what he wanted from me. I couldn't hide it forever, and if anyone had to know, I would rather it be Rift.

"My real name is Scandal Matthison. My father is William Matthison." Rift's eyes widened, and I didn't blame him. To realize that the girl you thought was just a slightly criminal sorceress was in fact the daughter of a notorious politician had to be a surprise. I didn't associate with my father, and never had. To hear that the man you know is your father denied you on live television by saying that he could not have produced an… I believe his exact words were "an unnatural creature". Yeah. Forgive me if I'm not exactly beating down his door to get him to attend family gatherings.

Logan clapped slowly. "There. That wasn't so hard, now was it?" He gestured for us to follow him, helped along by a shove in the back. I glared at the grunt behind us; Rift grabbed my wrist to jerk me out of the way of a massive cage, which I almost certainly would have run into due to my inattention. Once we were away from the altar, I breathed a little easier. We stopped in front of a rectangular wooden crate the size of a dinner table, filled to the brim with golden straw. An object roughly the size of a picnic basket was nestled in the center; Edgar lifted it with a soft grunt.

"This is the artifact that I mentioned. It has the power to create storms, ones large enough to flood half the country. One large enough to destroy this city would be a paltry thing." It didn't look like much, just a blue ball that had a subtle glow. I shouldn't have been able to feel anything, but there was a slight shift in my magic, the fine hairs on my arm standing up straight in salute. I couldn't quite feel it, but I knew it was there. It was like a limb had fallen asleep; tingly and distant, coming to life the more I flexed it. I shot a glance at Rift, whose handsome features were tight.

"You say that so casually, like you're not talking about obliterating a city of several million people." I really didn't want to talk to him any more than I had to, but whatever Rift was doing, his concentration was not something that Edgar needed to see.

Edgar shrugged and replaced the artifact in its down bedding of straw. I let out a breath as the lid was levered carefully into place, although I would have felt even better if they had nailed it into place. Some chains wouldn't be amiss. Maybe some cement, just to be safe.

"I suppose that this business has taught me that those that deserve to live will protect themselves."

I whistled, taking care to make it a little too loud for the indoors; everyone, including Rift, flinched, but there was a reason for the action: the too loud noise masked the click of the shackles opening.

"That's jaded," I said casually. Rift and I took care to stay as still as we could, but it was a struggle. Somehow he had managed to open the shackles. It couldn't have been with magic, and I hadn't seen any picks or pins, so I had no idea how he'd done it. Not that it mattered. However he'd done it, he had, and it opened up our options considerably.

"So what do you want with us? We have a theory."

This time it was Esther who spoke.

"We want to make an example out of you. Show people what happens to sorcerers who go against us, and to the cops who hunt us."

I swallowed thickly as she continued. "As soon as our men get back with your partners, then the fun can begin."

"*My* men," Edgar said with careful emphasis. "And just

in case you're wondering, I paid a lot of money to make sure that this warehouse is entirely magic proofed. None in or out."

"We weren't wondering," I lied, rattling the shackles a little to explain why. In fact I had been trying to send up a flare of magic since the moments the shackles had been unlocked; I'd discovered the magic proofing long before he mentioned it. If I had been able to send it up, we would have been found in minutes. One of the few sorcerers that worked for the police department, like I did, spent every day monitoring the city for large spikes of magic. It was often a sign of sinister or criminal activity. It definitely would have been this time.

After that, it lapsed into a tense silence, until our partners arrived. They climbed out of the backseat of the car and were led over to us.

"Still think this is a good idea?" Cara snarked.

"Now the fun begins." Rift and I were dragged bodily, not toward the altar as I had feared, but to one of the sturdy stone pillars. It stretched to the ceiling and was sunk deep into the concrete. Rift and I were roped to it, back to back. Cara and Elliott knelt in front of us. A camera on a tripod was positioned so that all of us were facing it. I turned my head to speak to Rift as our captors bustled around, no doubt in preparation for our imminent demise.

"I'm really hoping you have a plan."

"I sent up a flare ten minutes ago. We just have to hold out a little longer."

I frowned, working my wrist out of the shackle. "How? I couldn't get anything out when I tried."

"I'll explain later. Just hold on."

Edgar returned with something in his hand, the camera's

red light blinking behind him. I'd never minded being in front of a camera before, but right now, I would have given anything to be anywhere else.

"This is a Hunger." He showed us a tiny mechanical snake, carved with runes and no bigger than my index finger. My magic shook its head, and I pressed my back against the pillar, the ropes straining as I shifted as far away as I could. I didn't want that thing anywhere near me. Something about it was extremely sinister; the runes whispered of blood, betrayal, and pain. "It burrows under your skin and drains your magic, to be stored for later use. If it stays in long enough, your magic won't regenerate." Edith stood beside her son, a dark wooden box in her hand. As her son spoke, she turned a tiny key and opened the lid. Petite snakes like the one in Edgar's hand slithered within, lit up in various colors from the magic they contained, and my stomach lurched wildly. There was a soft click as Rift's neck cracked from craning it so hard.

"There you go." The snake lurched onto the bare skin of my forearm. Its skin was metallic and cool, scraping against my skin. A rune was drawn in the center of its back, a dark void of color. Long fangs appeared as it reeled back, then lunged forward. I shouted as it burrowed beneath my skin. I could see it wriggling, my skin shifting, and my stomach heaved. I sagged weakly against the pillar, biting my lip to keep from shouting again. I wouldn't give them the satisfaction; a taste liked I'd licked a penny filled my mouth, the tender skin of my lip tearing.

"Scandal, are you okay?" Rift's voice was pitched high with panic, but I could tell he was trying to be calm for my sake. I shook my head mutely, then realized he couldn't see me.

"No," I managed. It felt like a flaming scalpel was being dragged around beneath the surface of my skin, searing into my magic.

Edith and Edgar stepped back. "Look at the camera, please."

I leaned against the pillar for support, shaking my head and turning my face away. There was a grunt, not from me.

"That'll be enough waiting," Rift snarled. The shackle snapped as he yanked free, shedding the ropes. I sagged against the pillar, then pulled myself up. A vice of my magic tightened around Edgar and Edith, but I struggled to concentrate enough to hold it in place.

"Get it out of me," I gritted out. The tiny vermin was still shifting under my skin, the rune on its back pulsing as it fed on my magic. The pain was blinding.

Edgar was gasping, and I barely had the presence of mind to loosen my grasp. "Fine."

I released him and he tumbled to the floor. Hovering his hand over the snake's writhing body, he murmured a few words. The miniscule creature burrowed its way out, the rune on its back glowing indigo. Now that it was out, the pain receded, leaving behind a dull drum beat of misery.

Rift had thrown up a shield, bullets bouncing away. Edgar dropped the snake and I stomped on it, splattering metal and a shimmer of indigo. Edgar and Edith bound in my magic, we waited for the cavalry to arrive.

"Here," Rift said softly. He reached into the pocket of his jacket and produced a white handkerchief, his hands gentle as he wrapped it around my injured wrist. I couldn't help but crack a smile.

"Who even carries handkerchiefs anymore?"

He made a face at my good natured mocking. "But if I

didn't, you would be standing there bleeding on your jacket," he pointed out. I conceded the point, and we watched as armed men in enchanted riot gear burst in; the firefight on the other side was soon over. Rift cautiously lowered his barrier. Edith and Edgar were cuffed and taken away; Cara and Elliott were picked up, rubbing the raw skin of their wrists. The chief approached us, his face thunderous. I winced in preparation for the tirade I knew would follow, and he didn't disappoint.

"What on earth could you have been thinking? It was dangerous and unsanctioned. You could all have been killed, and even worse, you would have taken our best lead to Edgar Logan to the grave with you."

Rift seemed offended by the implication. "We almost died, but yeah, putting Logan in prison is clearly the most important thing here. We're fine, thanks for asking."

I stepped between them, holding my hands up. "How about we all just take a second to cool down. Rift, come on." He didn't move until I tugged on his arm, and then only reluctantly. "I could really use some medical attention." Rift followed me outside. All sorts of official vehicles were parked outside of the warehouse. There were several ambulances that I could have headed toward, but all of them seemed to be occupied; apparently the firefight outside of Rift's shield hadn't been as one sided as it had seemed. Instead, we hung back. Cara approached, Elliott hot on her heels. I tried to head her off before she could really get a full head of steam going.

"Look, we're really sorry, and we know it was stupid."

Rift jumped in as soon as I stopped to take a breath; despite the circumstances, I couldn't help but be impressed by how seamlessly we worked together. "We won't do it again, and we'll do whatever we can to make this better."

Cara held up a hand to stop up. "Just stop. This is so far over our heads right now, we can't even see daylight."

I swallowed hard as she held out her hand. "Give it." I didn't have to ask what she meant. I reached down slowly and unhooked my badge from my belt, trying not to laugh hysterically at the fact that it had stayed put through two kidnappings, only to be confiscated because we stepped over the line. There was a soft click as Rift detached his, placing it beside mine in Cara's palm.

"But that's not all, is it?" Rift asked softly. I could feel him shaking, and see the glint of magic on his fingertips as he struggled to keep it under control. I didn't blame him. This had been a taxing day for all of us.

"No. Unfortunately not. She reached into the pocket of her jacket and withdrew two cuffs. Not handcuffs, like I was getting all too used to seeing, but they may as well have been. These weren't just dampening cuffs, intended to slow our power. These were cuffs made for criminals, meant to cut off all access to magic for long periods of time. Tiny barbs on the inside would dig into our wrists, preventing us from taking it off without a key. Runes prevented outside magical intervention. Once these things were on, they weren't coming off without a key or a chainsaw.

Rift whitened. Elliott sighed, taking one of the cuffs and pulling Rift off to the side, leaving Cara and I alone. I couldn't help but stare at the cuff. Even when I'd been arrested before, I had never, ever, been put into a cuff like this. This was a permanent cuff. Ones just like this were used for prisoners with magic. There were rumors that being without access to their magic for long periods of time drove sorcerers insane, made them see spirits and the echoes of magic that had been performed before. I didn't want that to be us.

"Do we really have to do this?" More than anything else, I was sad. Rift and I had done the best that we could under the circumstances, and we were being treated like common criminals. No, worse than that, because these people knew us, knew that we hadn't meant any harm, and they had still chosen to tear us down like this.

"I'll get them off as soon as I can. It's just until the review clears." She cracked a pathetic smile. "The Captain thinks it might keep you two from doing something stupid."

I cracked a grin too, just as pale as hers. "We're teenagers. We don't need magic to do stupid things." Then it dawned on me. What specific thing did the Captain think that we were going to do that would warrant such extreme measures? The people that we had been chasing were here, as was the artifact that he had threatened the city with. There was nothing else to do, no other leads to chase down. So why did he think that we needed to be kept on a leash? "Wait a second. What does he think we're going to do?"

She sighed, her long fingers slipping through her hair. "I shouldn't tell you." She knew that, and I knew that, but we also knew that she was going to.

"Come on. It's only fair that I should know if it's something potentially life threatening." Her eyes flicked to the side and I winced. The part about my life being in danger had been at least partly in jest, but the fact that she wouldn't make eye contact meant that it wasn't a joke. She sighed deeply.

"We're still doing initial inventory of all the magical artifacts in the warehouse, but we have reason to believe that at least one of them is missing."

"What reason? And which artifact?"

"I can't tell you." She offered the cuff. My fingers curled as I reluctantly took it, then clipped it onto my right wrist. The spikes burrowed into my skin, so deeply that I imagined I could feel them scraping the bone in my wrist. My throat burned as tears pricked my eyes, but I refused to cry in front of everyone here. Already there were plenty of people staring, the agents from both our department and Rift's, along with the technicians responsible for cataloguing and recording all of the artifacts and creatures in the warehouse. No doubt there were some very interesting things in there, but I'd never get to see them. At the moment, it looked like I wasn't ever going to get a chance to redeem myself.

I lifted my eyes to Cara's, holding them strongly. "I want you to know that the only reason I put this cursed thing on is because I trust you. I trust you enough to leave myself at the mercy of others and cut myself off from the only constant in my life. I only wished you could trust me that much."

I turned on my heel and stalked away, heading for the darkest part of the city and the people that would welcome me there.

Chapter Ten

I felt bad leaving Rift behind, but right now, I could use some time alone to process what was happening, and if we were as alike as I thought we were, then he would welcome the same. The cuff was cinched so tightly that my wrist was throbbing, a dull ache that reminded me that I couldn't feel my magic. The worst part was that I wasn't completely cut off from it; I could feel it slightly, like something that was just out of reach. It was maddening, and I hated to think what it would do to me if I had to stay like this.

Pulling my sleeves down, I swerved toward the seedier part of the city, hugging the wall and heading toward a bar that was barely visible from the street. The neon sign above the door was flickering. I didn't make eye contact with any of the regulars as I stepped inside. I didn't think my arrival caused any commotion, at least until the bartender spoke, her voice strident and clear over the din.

"Sorceress."

I cocked an eyebrow at her, crossing my arms despite the pain it caused. One wrist was wrapped in a handkerchief and judging by the sluggish warmth, still bleeding slowly. The other had I-don't-even-want-to-think-how-long spikes embedded in it. Neither were particularly comfortable, but in a place like this, the appearance of being tough meant more than any pain it caused me.

"Bartender," I shot back with a smirk. She was a tall, lanky blonde with dark roots and fierce facial features. A white cloth used for drying glasses was in her hands, but she tossed it over her shoulder and slapped the counter. I went to her and she pulled me into a hug, half over the bar.

"Ouch, Aura, chill."

She stood back, holding me at arm's length. "I haven't seen you in months. I will not *chill.*" She was holding my wrist and I fought not to wince. Nevertheless, she noticed. She tossed the towel at the other bartender and switched her grip to my hand, towing me toward the back.

"We need to talk. Cover for me, will you?" This last she tossed at the other bartender as carelessly as she had thrown the towel; he rolled his eyes good-naturedly but nodded.

The door to the back room opened. It was full, but the patrons cleared out at a nod from Jessa. Not only was she the bartender, she was also part owner, and ruled this place like a queen. She sat me down at the poker table, paying no attention to the game in progress, and motioned for me to show her what was wrong with my wrist. I slid carefully out of my jacket and flipped it over the back of the chair, wincing as I did so. Her eyes flicked back and forth.

Apparently deciding the actually bleeding wrist was the more immediate problem, she started to unwind Rift's handkerchief from where it was wrapped around my wrist. It was stained with blood, the rust of the dried blood mixing with the fresh. The wound itself was nothing special to look at, just a short, vertical cut about an inch long. It was still bleeding sluggishly, but more concerning was the fact that the veins around it were glowing with my magic, but it was a dark, perverse color, too dark to be healthy.

"Okay, that's bad," I mumbled, poking the skin beside the wound with my fingertip. It only hurt when I touched the wound itself; the dark veins around it were numb, which was concerning in itself. I tried to light a spark to test if I could still use magic, not remembering that I was wearing a cuff. Aura didn't notice my temporary lapse in memory, but she did slap my hand away from the open wound.

"What's the matter with you? Don't touch that."

She took my wrist gently, lifting it to look at the cut. "What is this?"

It took me a second to remember what Edgar had called the evil little snake. "I think it was called a Hunger? It's this weird little snake thing that drains magic and stores it for later."

"Is it still in there?" she asked in fascination. I thought that was a bit of an odd choice of reaction for the situation, but I let it slide.

I shuddered. "No, thank goodness. Edgar took it out." I wiggled my fingers, but there was no magic to explain what I meant, not that she needed it. She was a sorceress herself, capable of altering moods. A handy trick for a bartender when her patrons got a little too handsy.

"And is Edgar...?" she trailed off, motioning absently.

"Edgar Logan, the notorious magical artifact smuggler? The very same."

"Alright. I'll be right back so we can take a look at that wrist, and you can tell me how you managed to run afoul of an artifact smuggler and ended up with a police-issue magical restraint cuff on your wrist." She motioned sternly. "You stay."

I made a face at her back as the door swung closed. "I'm beginning to feel like a dog." I wedged my fingers under the cuff and pulled, just to see how far it would come up, if at all. Good news is that it did come up. Bad news is that the enchantments in place didn't like that; the spikes lengthened, digging even deeper than before. I let go hastily. "Geez, sorry." To be honest, I didn't really want it off, at least not yet. I wanted to prove to the people in charge that I could be trusted, and that wouldn't exactly be helped if I pried off the cuff meant to… I honestly wasn't sure what it was supposed to be doing. It felt like a punishment for not doing what they said, but if I asked them, they would probably say something along the lines of "You broke our trust and we have to ensure that you aren't a danger to us or other members of the public." Not wrong, but I didn't have to be happy about it.

Aura came back in with a clean cloth, a tube of antiseptic, and a roll of sterile gauze. I held my wrist out for her to clean it, trying not to look at the strange darkness that seemed to be climbing my veins. She was careful with the wound, but she was still able to talk while she worked.

"So tell me what happened."

I contemplated what to say, or at least where to start. Probably best to start as close to the start as possible, when Rift had come into the picture. "A few days ago, a sorcerer named Rift that works for the government was paired with me. Our task was to create a shield over the entire city to trap Edgar Logan. After we had done that, all we had to do was wait." Now to the part that she wouldn't like. For all her toughness, Aura was one of my best friends from the city.

She was less a mother figure and more of an aunt figure, always there to help if I needed it but not intruding into my space, which I appreciated. Still, she was not going to be happy when we got to the part about kidnapping and everything else. "We, and our partners, were kidnapped by a group of bikers that were after the bounty on our head. I broke a curse on their leader and they let us go, which led us to the person who sold the magic shackles, and Edgar's mother kidnapped us. She tied us up with magic shackles and Edgar put the Hunger in my arm, but Rift broke the shackles and we escaped."

I took a breath. That pretty much covered our latest adventures; now there was only seeing what she had to say.

She exhaled slowly, tightening the bandage. "I honestly don't know how you manage to survive in this city on your own," she said finally. "And, I hate to say I told you so, but I did tell you that the police would turn against you someday."

I rolled my eyes. "It's not like I had a choice when I got arrested. There was nothing that my mom could do about it, and my dad sure wasn't going to help. I did what I had to do to stay out of prison." She pointed an accusing finger at me. She was sitting on the edge of the table, nearly in the cards still spread out.

"I offered to let you stay with us. You know, you're always welcome here. None of this would have happened if you had been here with us instead of the cops."

I rolled my eyes. "None of this would have happened, but who's to say something worse wouldn't have happened? If I can get into this much trouble with the law, can you imagine what I could do on this side?" She snorted, and my phone vibrated. I dug it out of my pocket, aware of Aura's wary eyes on me. I didn't want it to be Cara, and it wasn't. It was Rift, asking where I was and if I was okay? Sweet, but it made me wonder how he had gotten my number. If not from me, then likely from Cara, which meant that he was with her. I only hoped that he was okay, and that they hadn't locked him up or something.

I texted him back quickly. *I'm fine. Where are you?*

I came back to your apartment before Cara and Elliott could find me. They must still be at the crime scene or they'd be here already.

"Well, he can't stay there," I mused. "Pretty soon our partners will head back, and then there's no telling what they'll do with us."

"You're welcome to stay here," Aura offered, then sighed as she saw my expression. "But I know that you won't."

I hopped down, flexing my bandaged wrist, which was still surprisingly flexible despite the tight wrapping of gauze. "It's not fair for me to drag him into this and then leave him. We both made the choice to do what we did, but it's not fair for him to bear all the blowback." I shrugged into my jacket and headed for the door, then turned back to give her a hug. "Thank you for everything. I didn't mean to dump all of this on you; I just needed a place to lie low, with people that I can trust. This was the only place I could think of."

Aura squeezed me back, her smile sad. "You know that you're always welcome here."

"I know."

I headed back to my apartment, torn between hurrying to make sure that Rift was okay and not wanting to face whatever punishment was in store for us, which left me at a sort of anxious, half-hurry, which was fairly reminiscent of how I lived the rest of my life. My nerves were shot; I cast anxious glances at anyone who so much as looked at me, and quite a few who didn't. I debated on whether or not I could even stand being in the confined space of a taxi cab for long enough to get back to my apartment, decided it was better than giving everyone the evil eye while I walked the few miles, and picked the nearest cab. I told the driver my address and he nodded.

I checked my phone probably ten times in the fifteen minute drive back to my apartment. Rift hadn't mentioned anything about being hurt or, like, held captive or something, but then again, he wouldn't have been able to if was under duress, right? I didn't think Elliott would let anything happen to him, but then again, I hadn't thought that Cara would make me put on a magical restraint cuff. Sometimes the people we trust the most are the ones that make the sketchiest decisions.

I nudged my door open, poking my head cautiously around the frame. There were no voices, but that didn't necessarily mean anything. Rift was seated awkwardly on my couch, his long fingers fiddling with the cuff on his wrist. He didn't look any the worse for wear, other than dark shadows of exhaustion under his eyes. He straightened as I stepped inside, closing and locking the door behind me.

"I'm sorry for letting myself in. This is pretty much the only place that I've actually felt safe so far." He tilted his head consideringly. "Except for the little diner place, I guess."

I cracked a wan smile. "Yeah. My city hasn't exactly made a great impression on you, has it?"

"No. But you have." As soon as he said it, he glanced away, a flush creeping up his throat. "Sorry."

I tried to hide my own flush, startled at his sudden confession. We had bigger things to worry about at the moment, but we would definitely be revisiting this topic sometime in the near future. "How did you even get in here?" When I'd let us all in before, I had used my own keys, so it wasn't like he had seen me dig out the spare. Plus, it wasn't where most people would think to look for it. I had a small statue of a fox outside my door, as well as a flat welcome mat with classy swirls on it, both prime hiding places. Neither of them hid my key. My spare key was in the light fixture about my door; it would take magic or a ladder, as well as some tools, to be able to take it apart. It wasn't a typical place for a key to be hidden, and I doubted that he would have taken apart any visible spot to hide it to find his way in. With no magic to use, I was stumped as to how he could have gotten in.

"I have a confession to make."

That was ominous. I crouched, curiously inspecting the lock. "Look, if you picked the lock, I get it, but you could have just waited for me to get here."

He waved a hand and stood from the couch, practically vibrating with nervousness. His left hand gripped the hair at the top of his head, hard enough to look painful. I stood slowly, torn between wanting to comfort him and being very concerned about whatever it was that was making him act this way. "Take a breath. Whatever it is, it can't be that bad."

"I can use magic!" he blurted.

I squinted in confusion. "Yeah. So can I." I poked the cuff. "I mean, normally. That's kind of the point."

He barked a laugh. Some of the tension eased, and his shaking hands lowered. "That's not what I meant. Even with the cuff, I can still use my magic. Dampening spells don't work on me." My mouth gaped open as a sliver of magic worked its way between his fingers, not much but far more than I could manage at the moment.

"How?" I managed.

He shrugged helplessly, the magic disappearing. "I have no idea. That's the way that it's always been. And that's not all."

"What more is there, besides the fact that you could have freed yourself anytime you wanted and magic dampeners have no effect on you?" I was torn between irritation that he hadn't been honest with me and confusion as to why. If he had been able to free himself at any time, then why had he stayed? The only reason that I could think of was that he wanted to protect me, which was the only reason I wasn't having a full on meltdown right now.

Rift reached into his pocket and withdrew a piece of paper, folded into neat squares. He unfolded it and handed it to me. It was a printout of an email, and my eyes widened.

I see that you have captured my associate Mr. Logan. As much as I would like to congratulate you, unfortunately our business was not concluded, and therefore I must ask that you return him. If you do not, I will be forced to do something that we will both regret. I will begin to kill one person each hour until Mr. Logan is released, and one more each hour until the magical shield around the city is taken down. These people will be chosen at random and killed with magic, thus rendering any attempts that you may try at protecting the inhabitants of the city useless. As a sign of good faith, I will allow you to keep Ms. Logan. As I am aware that these things take time, I am willing to allow you twenty four hours to free Mr. Logan. The sands of time have already begun to fall.

Chapter Eleven

"Okay, what?"

Rift cracked a smile. "Right? That's what I thought too."

I stared at the paper in my hands, my mind whirling. I had so many questions, and some serious feelings. For one thing, this didn't explain why Rift hadn't told me about his strange ability, but it did put things into perspective. For another, I was getting real sick of people threatening us. The number of people threatening my city had jumped sharply since Rift had come, but I knew that was illogical. He'd come because of the bad guys, not the other way around.

I chose a question at random from the long list scrolling through my mind like a cat playing with a computer mouse. "How did you get this? *Where* did you get this?"

"When Elliott wouldn't answer me about why they were stripping our powers, I went over his head. I went back to the precinct and hacked into the evidence records. That showed up. It was sent twenty minutes after Logan was taken into custody, and ten minutes before they realized there was another artifact missing." He withdrew another paper, this one an aged drawing, and spread it on the table; his long fingers stretched the parchment tight so that we could see it better. "There's no name, but supposedly it can kill anyone, anywhere, with only the smallest bit of magic."

I ran my fingers through my hair, tugging at it in irritation. "Why hasn't this thing been destroyed already? This is a liability for like, everyone, everywhere."

Rift nodded in agreement. "It disappeared in the late 1800s and hasn't been seen again since it reappeared six months ago, where it jumped between three owners before becoming part of Logan's collection of ominous artifacts."

This was all too much to process. When in doubt, do the smart thing: find the comfort food. I kicked off my shoes and went to the cupboard, pulling down a bag of cheddar potato skins and offering some to Rift, which he accepted. My favorite meal was a chicken ranch bake, but I didn't feel like cooking, so chips and chocolate was the next best thing.

"So. What's our next move?"

Rift munched meditatively on the chips before he answered. "I think we should get our powers unbound first, or at least try. If we can get that done, we'll be much better prepared to face whatever is coming."

I nodded, sliding a chip clip onto the bag and tossing it loosely onto the counter. There'd be a few more chips in the bag after my roughness, but whatever. I grabbed my jacket, then paused.

"Is it just me, or did whoever wrote that sound a lot like the letter we got from "Edgar"?" I made sarcastic air quotes around the name. "Which means either Edgar had a letter written in case of his capture and has some sort of accomplice to send it to the precinct, or that someone else was pulling the strings this whole time."

Rift hopped down from the stool, slinging his jacket over one shoulder. He looked every inch a male model, but it was odd to see him without the badge hooked to his belt. Mine was missing as well, still in Cara's possession.

We walked to the precinct, our long strides eating up the distance. Everyone gave us a wide berth, which I thought was a bit rude but didn't seem to bother Rift at all. One of the other sorcerers from upstairs stopped us. He looked more like the stereotypical sorcerer than we did, with a long tan trench coat and lots of jewelry. People used to tease him about the trench coat, at least until the rumor had started that anything you needed was somewhere in those pockets. Trust me, once he pulled out a fork and stapler from the same pocket, you start to *believe*. No one had ever teased him about the jewelry because he had expensive taste.

"I heard about what happened, and I just wanted to say, it happens to the best of us. I've had my powers bound before, and the best thing to do is try not to reach for it."

As you can imagine, being told not to reach for your magic is somewhat parallel to being told not to look down while you're standing on a bridge over a fiery chasm. You weren't going to before, but now that someone told you you shouldn't, you definitely had to. As soon as I thought about not reaching for my magic, it made me think about the magic itself, and I was so conditioned to draw the magic out when I thought about it that…

"Thank you. We appreciate the support," I told him. He nodded, looking quite pleased with his show of support. The second he stepped away, I rolled my eyes. Rift snorted, his eyes glinting as he grinned crookedly.

"Got you too, didn't he?"

"Sure did." We had a good natured race up the stairs,

both of us taking two stairs at a time. We were evenly matched, but I was more competitive, so I may or may not have taken the inside corner before the floor we needed and cut him off. Panting, we sat on the hard stairs. Us showing up to show that we were serious teenage sorcerers panting and sweaty from racing each other up the stairs was a *wee* bit counterproductive. Not to mention that I needed a second to decide how I felt about things. Our lives were pretty much constantly in danger. We'd gone from kidnapping to attempted murder and back in the blink of an eye. Now my partner, whom I'd known for years, had bound my powers. I was terrified of what would happen if I was without it for any length of time, even more than I was of the bounty on our heads or the threat of mass murder in the city. On top of all that, there was Rift. I liked him, but more than that, I liked how he made me feel. He always had my back, and had multiple times had more confidence than I had in myself.

But before I could decide anything about Rift, there were other problems to solve. First, unbinding our magic. Whatever made him able to withstand the binding, I couldn't, and being without my magic was like having someone scratching a record on a player. You could ignore it for a while, if you really tried, but it was irritating and bad for everyone involved.

"Ready?" I asked. Rift nodded, holding out a hand to help me up. We rose together, the darkness of the binding cuffs stark against our skin. An irrational surge of jealousy filled me, envy that no matter what runes bound him, he still had access to his magic. My magic had been such a integral part of my life for so long that I hardly knew what to do without it. Through the worst times in my life it had been the one constant. Every breakup, every failed test, every fight with my mom, my magic had been there to help me through it. When I had been arrested and had my magic bound the first time, that had been the darkest and loneliest time in my life. I had felt cut off from everyone and everything, like my magic affected the way I saw the world and the way that I communicated with other people. All of that was different now.

Rift opened the door for me. "After you." I poked my head through the doorway. There on the left was the giant glass fish bowl of our office, but no Cara and no Elliott. Rift gave me a questioning look and I led the way to the Captain's office, where I rarely had occasion to venture. Even when I got yelled at, it was still normally in our big workspace, with all of us together. It was a rare occasion when I screwed up so badly that I got the privilege of being yelled at in private. The door was open, so I knocked.

A few seconds and a muffled conversation later, Cara's face appeared in the gap of the doorway. Her face hardened, but she opened it slowly. The Captain sat calmly on his side of the desk, with Elliott seated on our side and twisted around to face us. Rift lowered his head, his hair sliding forward into his eyes. Contrary to what most books for young adults would have you think, the longer hair didn't make him look tough and roguish; it made him look soft and young as he glanced up through his lashes. It stunned me how well a boy like this could hide the strength I had already seen from him.

"Hello, Captain," Rift said politely. The Captain arched his brows, beefy arms crossed.

"Where have you two been? You disappeared from the crime scene pretty quickly."

I fought the urge to snap back at him. Yes, I was irritated, but an attitude was not going to improve the situation. I could air my grievances later, when I wasn't powerless, in every sense of the word.

Taking a cue from Rift's calmness, I lowered my head and shrugged slightly. "I went for a walk. I just needed a chance to clear my head and figure out how I felt." None of which was a lie. I had gone for a walk to Aura's bar, although the way I had phrased it made it sound a lot more aimless and a lot less like I was keeping company with a few known felons. Also, I already knew how I felt before I left, but any kind of language that I could use to explain those feelings was not going to help our case.

The Captain was not going to fall for that. "And where did you go?"

I gritted my teeth. Lying would look better, but I had a feeling that he already knew and just wanted to see if I would tell him the truth. Either way, there was going to be blood. "I went to Aura's bar on the other side of the city."

His expression didn't change. "I know. I had a uniform following you because I was afraid you'd do something stupid. Turns out I was right. Show me your wrist."

I bristled, insulted by the insinuation that I had tried to have someone remove the cuff. It would have hurt, which I could deal with. As I had explained to Aura, I didn't want to break their trust, but right now, I wasn't feeling like there was much trust to break. I stepped closer and showed the Captain my wrist, trying to keep my expression neutral. His face changed as he decided that I hadn't tampered with it.

"I'm sorry. That was out of line."

"Yes, it was," Rift agreed, his voice cool. His head was tilted toward me and my eyes widened as I noticed the magic in his eyes. His posture, arms crossed and the long fingers of his right hand tucked under his elbow, were his attempt to hide the magic on his fingertips. It was still so strange that he wasn't bound by the cuff, but that was the only advantage that we had.

I hesitated, then touched his arm gently. The magic faded slowly. I met his eyes, watching the magic slowly leach, leaving the stunning blue behind, framed by his long lashes. Our reverie was shattered by the strident ring of the Captain's phone, the black landline on his desk that we all jokingly called "The Crisis Line". His eyes widened as he read the small Caller ID screen.

"Everybody out," he ordered. We hesitated, and he raised his voice sharply, punctuating the statement by stabbing one meaty finger at the door. "Out!"

Rift went first, tossing me a confused glance, now fully without magic within reach; I shrugged, equally confused. Cara was behind me, Elliott after her. He closed the door behind him. I turned to look at Cara, expecting to get yelled at, but her face was uncharacteristically grim.

"What's wrong?" I rubbed my wrist, choosing the one with the cuff since it hurt less. "Other than the obvious, I mean."

"I just saw the number on the Caller ID. The extension used by the state capital. Whoever was calling the Captain, they have some serious pull. Something is about to go down."

Chapter Twelve

Since nothing had actually been decided as to what was going to happen next, we all sat in the sorcery office, fingers drumming impatiently on the table. Elliott had gone to find coffees and hadn't come back yet. Rift was struggling not to show his magic, and I was struggling not to shout at Cara for asking me the same questions over and over.

"For the fifth time, Cara," I said through gritted teeth, "No, I don't know who would be calling from the capital. Your guess is just as good as mine."

"I doubt that. Isn't there anyone who you can think of that would want to help you from there?"

I snorted as I pretended to think about it. "Help? No. Advise the Captain to lock me up and throw the key into a rapidly flowing river? At least three people. Given an hour I could probably come up with a few more."

She made a face, fiddling with her badge where it hung on her belt. The badge was still there, but her gun and holster were missing. "There's no need to be sarcastic."

Rift's head shot up, his eyes darkening. I kicked him

lightly under the table; I knew him well enough by now to know that the color they were now warned that he was one step from magic. "That's where you're wrong. There is *every* need to be sarcastic. After all, that's our only defense right now." Very pointedly he raised his wrist to show the cuff. Purely out of curiosity I studied it more closely, wondering if there was something different about it that allowed him to use his magic. I should have known better. It was a department issue magic binding cuff, the kind that every member of the department carried, since one never knew when they were going to encounter someone with sorcery. It wasn't as if the department had the funds or the inclination to carefully search out different binding spells and cuffs for each sorcerer out there. It was a normal cuff, a perfect twin to the one on my wrist. The difference wasn't in the cuff itself, but rather in the sorcerer wearing it.

Cara opened her mouth to protest, but the soft chime of a group text on all of our phones startled us. *Go home. There's someone who wants to speak with you.* I squinted at the number. If I remembered correctly, that was the Captain's number, although I had never known him to send a text to anyone, let alone a group text. Just to verify the number I scrolled through my contacts; sure enough, it matched the number listed under *Captain.* We weren't allowed to call him by his actual name. Honestly, I probably couldn't have thought of it right off hand.

Rift and I stood, throwing on our jackets.

"Where are you going?" Cara asked.

I waggled my phone back and forth. "When someone in charge tells me to go home, I go home, especially when staying damages my chances of getting my magic unbound. Rift and I are going back to my apartment to mope about our lost magic and drown our sorrows in ice cream and ramen noodles." Rift made a face at the combination and i rolled my eyes at him. They were the first two foods that I could think of; it wasn't my fault that they weren't exactly palatable together. "And you can go wherever you want and do whatever you want. You are, after all, an adult."

I stalked toward the door, catching her shocked expression in the glass. I knew I was being unkind and that she didn't deserve it but for right now it was best for her to stay from us. She was a very good detective, but she had chosen a fine time to be by the book. It would be too hard for us to investigate this new threat if she was following us around. For right now, she had to stay mad at me.

Rift's long legs carried him to the door before I reached it. His forearm tensed as he opened it, leaning on the edge to get enough leverage. I nodded shortly, but offered a smile to soften the expression. He hung back at my shoulder.

"I still don't know my way around as well as I should," he explained. "Would you show me around?"

I wanted to, but not now. There were too many people around shooting us dark glances and concerned glances at the cuffs on our wrists; I would much rather do it later, when there was no one around but the slow tempered night shift to see us. Plus, anyone powerful enough to make the Captain stop in the middle of his tirade wasn't someone that I wanted to keep waiting.

I crossed my arms and glared at the person standing below where we stood on the steps, leaning smugly against the shining black of a long limousine. "You."

Chapter Thirteen

"Me," my father agreed calmly. His tailored suit was deepest navy, expensive cufflinks visible below the sleeves. His brown hair, so like mine, was cut just long enough to be brushed back from his face, slicked into place with some sort of liquid. Tanned skin and straight white teeth perfectly matched every campaign poster and billboard with his face on. Everything about him screamed money, power, and lies.

"What are you doing here?"

"Is that any way to speak to your father?" he asked chidingly. His polished wingtip shoes flashed as he ascended the stairs toward us smoothly, as if he had all the time in the world.

I made a show of looking around, squinting. "I don't see any fathers here. Do you, Rift?"

Rift arched a dark brow but made the wise choice not to comment.

Senator Matthison placed a hand on his chest, to the right of his expensive silk tie, feigning hurt. "I'm hurt. I haven't seen you in years, and this is how you treat me after I save you?"

I held up a finger. "Wrong. I have never, in my life, seen your person. I have, however, been subjected to the excruciatingly long video of you explaining to every reporter in the city how you regretted your time with my mom, especially since it created an "unnatural creature that does not belong on this earth," I snarled. Out of the corner of my eye, I saw Rift's look of horror, his eyes wide. I stalked down the steps toward my father. I was sick and tired of being pushed around and being bullied because he didn't like what I was. I had no choice in being a sorceress, but more than that, I wasn't ashamed of it. I did good work and used my power for good. If he couldn't accept that, then the problem was with him, not with me.

I was going to tell him everything that had been building up in all the years that I had never seen him, and then I would be content to never lay eyes on him again in my life. "Kids at school used to play that video all the time. They said that if my own father didn't want me, then who else would? The boy I had a crush on told me that in high school, right before he put a rumor out that I..." I swallowed. Nope. Different train of thought, right now. "But my personal favorite is the time when they put that video up behind me when I was running for student body president." I took a slow breath. Rift's hand was warm and soft on my shoulder as he gave me a reassuring squeeze, reminding me that he was here for moral support.

My father's face softened, completely at odds with the arrogant facade that he presented to the world. He stepped closer and I tensed as I stood my ground. "I'm sorry for everything that I said about you. I didn't know you, and somehow that made it easier to look into those cameras and read the words that they wanted me to say."

I crossed my arms in disbelief. Then quickly uncrossed them, because both wrists still hurt and being dramatic wasn't worth it. "That's really nice, but how does it help me?"

"I'm sorry," he repeated. "But my first step toward making amends was getting the Captain off your back and at least giving you a chance to get your powers back."

I frowned in confusion. "What do you mean "a chance"?" I asked. "I thought this was like every other time. They do a review, figure out that we did what we had to do, and then unbind our magic." That's how it had always been before. None of the sorcerers that I knew had ever had their magic permanently bound, although it was possible. They would just have to do something a lot worse than what we had done. At least, I thought so.

The Senator shook his head. "This time the disciplinary committee has different members. They say that you failed in your mission and that you used your magic in an offensive manner, thus putting the department at risk."

"That's crap," Rift said sharply, startling me with his vehemence. "We did everything that we could, and now we're being punished for it."

My father nodded slowly. "I agree." He turned to look at me, his eyes soft. "Whatever my failings, when I heard about what they were going to do to you two, I knew I had to stop it." This entire time we had been slowly moving down toward his limo, in part because of all the stares we were getting, standing in the middle of the steps and having a spirited, if quiet, argument. I was not going to get in, but at least we had a little bit of cover.

"So what are we going to do?" Rift asked. He was still wary of my father, shoulders tense and gaze challenging, but his body angling toward me suggested that he was deferring to my judgement. The problem was, I wasn't sure my judgement could be trusted in this particular case.

"There'll be a petition. You have to get so many signatures, people that would be willing to step in front of the committee and say that you're decent kids who don't deserve to have your magic bound." He reached into his jacket and handed me two pages, filled with tiny lines for signatures, and my heart sank. I didn't even know this many people, and I certainly didn't know this many people who would step in front of a legal proceeding and say that I was a good person. In fact, most of them would probably say the opposite.

"I'll do my best to help you, but you have to your best. You have forty eight hours before these have to be presented in front of the people in charge. If you don't make it, your magic will likely be bound in a more permanent fashion."

A call rang on his cell phone, and with a soft apology, he retreated into his limo and drove away. I hugged myself as we descended the stairs slowly, trying to wrap my head around things. My magic was now dependent on the opinions of others; somehow, all the events of my life, both good and bad, had boiled down to a popularity contest. One that I had to win, or else my life would change forever.

Chapter Fourteen

The next two days passed in a frenzy of activity. Rift and I rolled out of bed at the crack of dawn to start getting signatures, the pages full of empty lines taunting us. We started at the station; nearly everyone signed. Even the ones who didn't particularly like me didn't think that my magic should be bound, which was both surprising and flattering.

We pounced on the secretaries first, then the officers finishing with their morning briefing; the theory was that a cop full of donuts and coffee, with no bad experiences in the day yet, would be more likely to sign than if we asked them at the end of their shifts. We even grabbed a few of the people being booked, one of whom was so drunk that he could hardly hold the pen. I felt a little bad about that one, but as Rift pointed out, there was no rule stating that the signatures had to be from someone sober. Loopholes, kids.

Once we were finished at the station, we headed outside, to rustle up some signatures on the street. Most were too busy to pay attention to what they were signing; they just scribbled a signature and motioned for us to go away which, while not exactly flattering as to how much we mattered in the grand scheme of things, did count toward our totals. The lines slowly began to fill, and for most of the first day, I had the cautious feeling that we might be able to make it, a feeling that lasted into my dreams that night.

That feeling didn't last long during the second day. Few people wanted to sign, and even fewer seemed to care. We were down to the last hours, and we still didn't have enough. Dejected, Rift and I headed back to my apartment, picking up some junk food to eat because neither of us felt like cooking.

I sat on my kitchen counter, slurping dejectedly on flavored noodles. Rift was sitting on the kitchen stool like a normal person, even if his legs were crossed on a surface that shouldn't have allowed that. He was also eating his noodles with the chopsticks that they had come with, whereas I had grabbed a fork as soon as we'd come in.

"So now what?" I asked. The pages were on the counter. There were only about twenty signature lines left, but we had less than two hours until we had to present the signatures for the hearing, and twenty suddenly seemed like a totally unreachable number for that amount of time.

Rift shrugged helplessly. "I'm several hundred miles from anyone I know. Is there anyone else you can think of that would sign?"

"A few people here and there, but not enough to make a difference. By the time we track them all down, it'll be too late." I thought of all the people that I had helped in the past. They might sign, but there was no guarantee that we would find them in time.

Rift unfolded his lanky frame from the stool, gulping the last of his noodles.

"Then there's no time to waste. Let's go."

We headed across the city to the first people that I could think of: Ernest and his wife, Moon's owners. I could only hope that they would sign, which I thought they would. I was too nervous to knock on their door, so Rift did it for me.

Soft barks from inside, muffled by the thick wooden door and I grinned. Rift smiled too, teeth flashing, as the door opened. Ernest's eyes widened. "Scandal! How unexpected to see you." He blanched, obviously realizing how that sounded. "I'm sorry. That was rude. I didn't mean that the way it sounded."

Moon barked, scratching at my leg. I crouched to scoop her up, offering a smile to Ernest. "It's fine. I didn't think that's what you meant."

His wife appeared, poking her head over her husband's shoulder, her face lighting up when she saw me. "Scandal! How nice to see you." She smacked Ernest's arm gently, clearly both fond and frustrated. "Why didn't you invite these nice young people inside? Don't be rude." She tugged him back, allowing us to enter. "Come in."

Once the door was closed behind us, Ernest's wife held out her hand for Rift to shake. He did, his long fingers engulfing her slender ones. I felt awful that I didn't even know her name. Here I'd come to ask a favor, and I couldn't even ask her by name. I made a silent promise to be more attentive in the future. The night that I'd brought Moon back, I had been tired and cranky, not to mention filthy, but that was no excuse for my behavior.

"Hello, young man. My name is Ethel."

Rift nodded, shaking his hair out of his eyes and offering a soft smile. "My name is Rift, ma'am."

Moon barked to be let down. I lowered her to the floor,

already flushing as I thought of how best to go about asking them to sign our petition. They only knew me as the girl that had brought their lost dog back. If I told them that my magic was bound, they would want to know why, and I would have to explain the situation as best as I could. No doubt they would think less of me.

"And who are you, young man?" She squinted at Rift in mock suspicion, nose crinkling. "Are you her boyfriend?"

I waited, curious to hear how he would respond. Most guys would have jumped and said no immediately, deeply embarrassed that someone had connected them to a sorceress, even if it wasn't true. Instead, Rift's soft smile continued as he tucked his hair behind his ears. "No. We're only working tomorrow right now."

Ethel's silver brows rose, mouth quirking. I don't think any of us missed the phrasing, and my heart pounded a little faster when he turned to look at me. I stared, dumbfounded, for a solid ten seconds before it occurred to me that he had given me a perfect opening to ask our favor and I was just letting it slip away while I was gawking. I shook myself.

"We need a favor." I held up my wrist, showing the one with the cuff. The other was still bandaged, but luckily, neither Ethel nor Ernest asked about it. "Right now, this cuff means that our magic is bound. We have to have a certain amount of signatures to present at a hearing in," I checked my watch, swallowing hard. "Just over an hour. We need twenty more signatures. Ideally, people that would stand up at the hearing and say that they don't believe we would intentionally harm someone with their magic." I took a slow breath, trying to calm my racing heart as the older couple thought through our request.

Ethel clapped her hands, startling Rift and I. Out of the

corner of my eye I saw a flare of magic from his startlement, and hurriedly grasped his hand to hide the color. His eyes flicked toward me, but no one commented.

"Twenty, you said?" I nodded mutely. She went to the telephone on the wall, an old fashioned rotary phone in a pretty pearlescent color that blended in perfectly with the decor. "We've got work to do then." She picked up the phone, already dialing. "Darling, why don't you use the phone in the kitchen to call your poker club and call an emergency meeting of the poker club? If they don't want to come, tell them I'll make pecan pie."

Ernest nodded excitedly, Moon barking as she chased him around the corner. Rift backed into the doorway behind him, mouth open in quiet fascination that I shared.

"Are we about to be saved by a poker club and a bridge club?"

Ethel smiled. "Of course, Marge. I'd love to see pictures of your new cat as soon as we finish our business." The phone chimed gently as she hung up. "Well, the plan is in motion. The rest of our clubs will be here in ten minutes. I can't make any promises, but I'm sure they'll want to help."

Chapter Fifteen

I stared out at the sea of expectant faces and swallowed nervously. Rift squeezed my hand comfortingly, and I steeled myself to tell my story to the crowd.

Ernest belched and he clapped his hands over his mouth in horror. Ethel rolled her eyes. "Go on, dear. They're ready to hear your story."

Feeling bolstered by her quiet confidence, I nodded. "Rift and I are sorcerers who work with the police to solve crimes. There was a series of unfortunate events, and now our magic is bound. We need twenty signatures of people to say that we deserve to get our magic back." In the interest of full disclosure I added, "And you may be called to testify at the hearing tonight."

Very deliberately, Ernest took a pen and signed both of our papers. Ethel kissed his cheek and took the pen, adding her scrawling, elegant signature beneath his. Marge hesitated.

"Why should we? No offense, but we don't know you. Why should we put our support behind two teenagers that might very well deserve what they're about to get?"

I swallowed hard, but Ethel spoke first. I expected her to call on their friendship, as obviously they were a tight knit group. Nope. She went right for the heart. "Because Scandal is the young lady that brought Moon back to us." Marge didn't even blink. She took the pen from Ethel and signed neatly, sliding the pages on to the next person.

"Why didn't you just say so?"

I laughed, slightly hysterically. Ethel sent us into another room to rest while the rest of the signatures were filled out, and I was all too happy to oblige. I flung myself down on the couch. I was shaking visibly, so relieved that I could practically taste my magic. Rift folded himself onto the floor in front of me. He frowned when he saw my shivers.

"Are you cold?" I nodded slowly. Technically yes, I was a little cold, although that wasn't the main reason that I was trembling. His magic slithered to his fingertips, periwinkle blue that subtly warmed my fingers. His hands were warm on mine. Strangely enough, I could see the magic under his skin, as if it were physically flowing through his veins. It seemed to hesitate where the dampening cuff was, darkening for a moment before continuing to where he sent it. My first instinct was to reach for my own magic, although logically I knew that I couldn't reach it; to my shock, Rift's magic leapt to my command. He yelped, muffling the sound almost immediately. I cringed back, the magic disappearing.

"I'm sorry. Did I hurt you? I didn't mean to do that. I was reaching for mine, and then it was yours, and then…" I babbled. He sat back, staring at his own hands in surprise.

"You didn't hurt me. I was surprised, is all." He glanced up suddenly, eyes shining. "Can you do it again?"

I balked. I hadn't meant to do it the first time. Judging by both of our reactions, I hardly thought it a good idea for me to do it on purpose. "Why?"

"Because I want to know why you can reach my magic. It doesn't feel like you're taking it away from me, like it has other times. It feels like…" He groped for words. "Like it likes you. Like it's coming to you because it wants to, not because you're making it. Go ahead." He nodded encouragingly.

I closed my eyes, feeling his hands in mine, then reaching beyond that. In my mind's eye, I could see the magic shining in Rift's chest like an invitation. I reached for it like my own magic, calling gently as an invitation. It came eagerly. I opened my eyes, staring at the magic winding through my fingers like a cat asking to be petted. Rift's eyes met mine and I jolted, startled at the violet in his eyes, as if he was channeling my magic, except there was no magic to channel at the moment. I released his magic with a gasp.

As strange as I felt having channeled someone else's magic when I couldn't even channel my own, it was nothing compared to how Rift must have felt. He doubled over, his head between his knees. I slid off the couch, my hands hovering uncertainly. I wanted to touch him, but I was afraid to. I mustered my courage and touched his back, slow strokes more to comfort me than him.

"I'm sorry. I did it again."

He raised his head, sweat matting his thick hair to his face. His cheeks were flushed like he had a fever, his eyes shining. "It was my fault. I asked you to. I just didn't expect that."

"What happened?" I asked softly.

When he spoke, his voice was muffled. "I think we switched magic for a second there."

I paled, my gut wrenching. "And since mine's not there, I took yours and you got nothing. I'm so sorry."

"My fault. Interesting experiment that I'd prefer not to repeat." He tried to sit up and swayed. Other than the pink on his face, he was ghostly pale. I didn't have to be touching him to realize that he was very sick. "Can I lean on you?" he asked. I nodded and he leaned against my shoulder, his hair brushing the side of my neck. His long lashes brushed his cheekbones as his eyes fluttered closed.

Ethel poked her head in, our papers clutched in her hand. Her dark brows rose and I flushed, but Rift didn't know that she was there, so I wasn't going to move until he realized. Ethel cleared her throat softly.

"You have all your signatures. We thought we might drive you to the hearing. Just in case you need backup."

Rift sat up, gripping my arm for support as I helped him stand. "Thank you, Ethel. We appreciate that."

Ethel frowned at Rift, who was leaning on my arm. His color was returning, and he finally straightened up. "That would be great, thank you."

"Are you alright?"

He nodded. "Just a little dizzy for a minute. I'll be fine."

"Well, let's get going then." She herded us toward the door, gathering up Ernest and their other friends on the way out. I frowned at the minivan parked on the street outside. It would fit a few of us, but certainly not all of us, unless the older folks were willing to get involved in a car cram. I was sure that Ethel had already thought of that, but I wanted to voice my concern just in case.

"Umm, Ethel?" I said softly. "Where is everyone going to sit? The minivan wasn't meant for this many people."

She chuckled and pointed down the block. "Only the four of us are going to ride in the van. The others have a transit van that they use to get around. They'll meet us at the courthouse."

I nodded; that made more sense. Ethel's friends split off toward the white can down the block, while Ernest scrambled into the driver's seat with a maniacal laugh. Ethel rolled her eyes.

"We always argue over who gets to drive. He drives like a turtle, and he claims that I have a lead foot," she said primly, emphasizing the *claims*. She took the shotgun seat, while Rift slid open the sliding door in the back, motioning for me to climb in first. There was one seat on each side, with a narrow aisle in the middle leading back to a three seat bench. I took the seat on the far side; Rift climbed in and slid the door closed.

None of us spoke as traffic inched toward the courthouse. The transit van was easily visible behind us, chugging placidly along no matter how many cars wedged their way between us. Ernest wove through the city, then turned into the parking structure across the street from the courthouse. He handed over a few dollars to the till manager, and parked on the lowest level. We all piled out, meeting the others as they climbed much more slowly out of the transit van.

"Well, let's go then," Marge said in irritation as I checked my watch anxiously. The walk across the street had been uneventful; no one had gotten hit by a car, we had all made it, and now we were waiting patiently for the doors of the courtroom to open. I could still feel residual effects of Rift's magic; it slipped anxiously under my skin. He looked infinitely better now than he had before, with his color back and the sweat missing. He was still leaning on my shoulder, but that was more from choice than necessity.

"We'll be fine," he whispered.

"I hope so," I whispered back. According to my watch and the clock on the wall, our hearing should have started ten minutes ago. Ten minutes isn't long when you're at work or playing a board game, but it sure is when you're waiting to hear whether your magic is going to be permanently bound. The doors finally opened and I shot up, but the crowd exiting in the courtroom was pretty much a stampede; there was no point in trying to get in until they all cleared a path. Finally there was enough room for us to leave the bench and head in. There was a long panel at the front, just below where the judge would have sat in a typical trial. Five men and two women waited, shuffling papers in thick portfolios. A glass of water sat in front of each, along with a pitcher of water. There was no bailiff, but I had no doubt that these people were more than capable of defending themselves.

I glanced uncertainly at Rift. Ernest, Ethel, and the rest of the powerfully aged wonders had seated themselves in the viewing gallery, but there were no chairs for us to sit in, so we stood in front of the panel. I twisted my hands, then chided myself and forced them to my sides. Something like that would make them think that we were guilty, and that wasn't an image I wanted to project. I mean, yes, technically we were guilty, but we'd only done what we had to do. That was what we had to explain to them.

The woman in the middle spoke. "Do you have your petitions?"

We nodded like marionettes on strings. I nearly had a

heart attack when I reached into my jacket and didn't immediately feel my page, but it had only slid a little further into the lining. Rift, of course, knew exactly where it was and produced it confidently.

"May we see them?" I laid it carefully on the table in front of her, as did Rift. She inspected them. There were more than enough signatures; the dark lines of ink continued even where there weren't spaces provided. A slow nod.

"It seems to be in order. However, we'd like to hear your side of the story before we make a final decision."

It seemed to occur to her that we were still standing there awkwardly. Her face softened. "There are some chairs behind you." Rift retrieved them, placing mine neatly behind me before he seated himself. I heard Ethel titter and fought down the urge to grin at her giddiness. I too was impressed by his manners, but now wasn't the time.

"So tell us what happened." Which part? The part where we'd built a massive magical working, the part where our own partners had locked us up, the part where we'd been kidnapped, or the part where we'd done something very dangerous and stupid but had at least managed to catch a criminal? I decided to start nearer to the end; they didn't seem patient enough to hear the whole story.

"We had an opportunity to apprehend a criminal handed to us on a silver platter. We were reasonably convinced of our success, and leaving our partners behind was the only way to accomplish that goal. It was no different than any other undercover operation."

"Except for the fact that you willingly consented to be kidnapped." I winced. The worst part was that she was right.

"And haven't other officers consented to the same thing

in the past?" Rift offered reasonably. Slow nods from the committee. One point for Rift.

"We understand. And how would you expect us to react to the accusation that you did, in fact, use your magic with force?"

My turn. "Yes, we did use it with force, but it wasn't *deadly* force," I pointed out. "Plus, we were only trying apprehend a criminal. We didn't use any force not necessary to protect ourselves and accomplish that goal."

The committee nodded. "Give us a moment to deliberate, and we'll give you our decision."

My heart climbed into my throat as they spoke in low voices, faces turned away so that I couldn't even read their lips. Rift grasped my hand under the table; it tightened as they spoke.

"We've made a decision. In light of the signatures that you've collected, as well as the testimony that you've given, we have determined that having your magic bound is unnecessary and may very well be counterproductive. You can leave here and head back to the police station with this paper," she held up a sheet. "And your magic will be restored to you. All charges have been dropped. You are free to go. "

Chapter Sixteen

After we'd done a round of hugs and congratulations with the well aged wonders, Rift and I set off toward the station. It was only a few blocks away, and a walk to clear my head didn't sound too bad right now. We descended the steps of the courthouse and swerved left. It was an unbelievable feeling to know that I was just minutes away from getting my magic back. Rift walked lighter too; I knew it must have been weighing on him to pretend that he didn't have magic, to hide it when he normally could have shown it. Otherwise he risked people learning about his strange gift, which could put him in danger. Not to mention the fact that we could switch magic, which was something I'd never been able to do with anyone else before.

Sharing magic with someone was one thing. Yes, I'd done that with Rift, but I'd also done it with others before him and would likely do it with others after. Sharing magic was still my magic; I was just lending it to someone else, allowing them to weave it into their own magic to make the spell stronger. That wasn't what had happened with Rift earlier.

Honestly, it shouldn't have been *able* to happen. I hadn't just shared his magic; I had reached inside him and drawn it as I would draw my own, and for those brief few moments, he would have been able to draw mine. My mind swirled with all the things that we could do with this newfound talent, but we'd have to try again later to learn more about it. At least, if Rift wanted to. If he wanted to leave it alone after his nasty experience, I wouldn't blame him.

"So what are you going to do with your magic, once you get it back? Are you going to keep it to yourself, or are you going to use it to make toast?"

I laughed. I knew he meant I would be able to use it for small, mundane tasks like I was used to, but I had to laugh at his choice of example. "You know what I'm sick of?"

He blinked, startled by the topic change. "What?"

"I'm sick of all this magicky angst. Being kidnapped, having my magic drained and then bound. I'm done. I just want to use my magic for something fun before we go back to being all serious and crime solving."

"So what do you want to do?"

"I haven't decided yet," I said primly. He laughed.

After that, we walked in slow silence. Rift didn't know where in the station we had to go, and he seemed content to follow my lead. I swerved around the back alley. The door was open, but I still knocked. The woman inside had massive glasses; when she blinked, she looked like an owl. I'd met her only briefly, but I knew who she was.

"Hi, Izalia," I said softly, trying not to startle her. It didn't work; she jolted back with a startled yelp, deep yellow magic flaring on the fingers that caught the edge of the counter. I placed the piece of paper from the committee on the counter slowly; she picked it up, her eyes flicking as she read it.

"Yay!" she burst out, all but throwing herself over the counter to give me a hug. I rocked back in surprise, my hands rising to pat her back awkwardly. We didn't really know one another all that well, so I was rather startled at this display of enthusiasm. She flushed as she drew back, folding her hands and looking down.

"I'm sorry," she said softly. Her posture and voice made me look more closely at her; she couldn't have been more than a few years older than me, in her early twenties. Her youth made the sudden enthusiasm more probable. "Sometimes I get a little excited."

Rift laughed, startling us both. He waited until she lifted her head, then flashed a stunning grin that made her shoulders relax. "Don't worry. We're excited too. Right, Scandal?"

I nodded, smiling as well. "Right." I leaned closer like I was sharing a secret, my left hand braced on the counter for support; pain rocketed through my wrist, where the Hunger had been, but I tried to ignore it. "Besides. We could all use a little excitement sometimes. Gets the blood pumping."

Rift rolled his eyes as Izalia turned away, humming softly. We'd had more than our fair share of excitement these past few days, and sometimes it was hard to remember that I'd only met him... two days ago? Three? I couldn't even remember. It felt like I'd known him my whole life, but that could have been us bonding our magic so many times. Even now I could feel it winding over the skin of my hands, like it was saying hello. My left wrist throbbed, but I wasn't going to take the bandage off to check it.

"So how does this work?" I asked. Izalia turned, holding a glowing key.

"I unlock the shackles and you get your magic back."

I sighed. "All that work and stress for two minutes."

She nodded, still holding the key. "Just a fair warning though: you might feel a little weak and ill as your magic comes back. It's totally normal, just your body getting used to having magic again after it's been missing for a while."

"It's only been a few days, but okay," I said doubtfully. Yellow magic glowed on her fingers as she hovered over the shackle; a small lock appeared on the top, into which she inserted the key. The shackle dropped to the ground with a rather anticlimactic clang. My magic rushed back, and I thought hazily that I should have believed her. I was vaguely aware of her unlocking Rift's shackle; past that, I was focused on the magic. It seemed to fill all the cracks in my being, filling my body until it felt like I was going to explode. I tried to pull it back, coax it back to where it should be, but it was too slow. Pain radiated through my muscles and I cried out as it hit the wound in my wrist from the Hunger.

A hand touched my arm gently, too large to be Izalia's. If Rift was saying something, I couldn't hear him past the pain. The blue of his magic appeared behind my eyes. It wound around my magic, blunting the edges and pulling it back so it no longer felt like I was being torn apart from the inside out. Slowly my magic receded to its place in my chest, with a final burst like a goodbye to Rift's magic. I opened my eyes, finally aware enough to take in my surroundings.

Rift was crouched in front of me and offered a smile when he noticed my eyes were open. Izalia had retreated to the corner of the room to give us privacy. Rift's cuff lay on the table next to mine. I took a shaky breath.

"Thanks for that," I mumbled. I still felt shaky and weak, but I wasn't in pain anymore. "I don't know what would have happened if you hadn't done that."

He expelled a breath. "I don't know either, and I don't

want to find out." He straightened and I held my arms out for a hug, then changed my mind and kissed him quickly on the cheek. His eyes widened and I flushed.

"Well, isn't that just the sweetest." I spun, startled. A man stood in the doorway, a long black trench coat sweeping the floor. Frizzy brown curls swayed against his shoulders, but most striking of all was the black leather patch over his left eye. If not for that, he would have looked like an artist, one of those that you saw on busy sidewalks with a sign that read *College student drawing caricatures. Small donations accepted and encouraged.* With the patch, he looked more like a pirate king looking down on his subjects. My magic was slow and sluggish when I called to it, like it was cowering. Taking the hint, I focused instead on pushing it down, of hiding any sign that I had it back. Izalia had disappeared but Rift was very much present, magic rippling aggressively in his hands.

"Who are you and what do you want?"

The man laughed indulgently. "I think you both know who I am. After all, I have contacted you before. You don't need anything to call me, but you may call me The Barkeep, if you must. As to what I want, for right now I only want to speak with you."

"Why? What could we have to say that would interest you?"

He clicked his tongue. "You underestimate your interesting qualities. Two teenage sorcerers with no training who managed to build a working around an entire city, built to keep in only one man? You two are certainly enough to keep me entertained."

"You want to steal our magic," I guessed. He frowned, his eyebrows drawing together. Clearly he didn't appreciate me stealing his thunder, but I just wanted this, whatever this was, to be over with quickly.

"No. Stealing is beneath me. I want you to give it to me freely."

Rift snickered. "No chance, buddy."

"What will you give us if we do?" I asked shrewdly. "What incentive do we have?"

The Barkeep straightened. "What do you want?"

"I want you to leave this city and never come back. Neither you nor anyone you know will contact Rift or anyone we care about in any way, ever."

"And you will give me your magic?" His eyes were hungry, the pale blue glittering. He hadn't seen my magic so he didn't know I had it back, but I had another idea in mind.

"There's only one problem with that. My magic is bound. I would give it to you, but it's gone."

He motioned to the room we were in, and I swore silently. If he knew what this room was for, as he clearly did, then this was going to be harder than I thought. "Rift has his, but since he's not going to give his up, I guess you'll have to settle for mine."

Rift and The Barkeep shot me identical looks of confusion. I tried to keep the smirk off my face; that was not an expression someone in my situation should be wearing. Instead I tried to look as devastated as possible. It wasn't hard; fear was pretty close to sadness, and there was plenty of fear to go around.

"I thought you said…"

"I did." I reached into my pocket and retrieved a small metallic object. Rift's eyes widened when he saw the Hunger, swallowing convulsively. I didn't blame him, especially since I could still see my magic glowing inside of it. "This is a

Hunger. It steals and stores magic for later use. This is the last of my magic that anyone will ever see. It's yours, if you agree to the terms I set before."

The Barkeep tapped his chin with a long finger. I could see his brain working, so I took it just one step further. "You seem like a pretty discerning man. Just think: this is the last of my magic. If you describe our accomplishments, people will know what you have is one of a kind. That makes it worth even more."

That decided him. "Fine. One of your magic is better than none. I agree with your terms. Now hand it over so I can be on my way."

He held out his hand for the Hunger. All I wanted to do was chuck it at his face and tell him not to let the door hit him in the butt on the way out, but I held it out of reach. "And you won't hurt us?"

"I'm offended that you think so little of me." I arched a brow and he sighed. "No. Now give it."

I handed it to him. With a slow, exaggerated bow, he ghosted out the door. Rift's magic finally overflowed, shattering a small glass on the far side of the room before he could rein it in. He flushed darkly. "Why would you do that? Where did you get it?"

"Why, because it was the best option and nobody got hurt. Where, the evidence lockup, where I still had access to even with my powers revoked. When, a question that you didn't ask, this morning, when I left my apartment early."

"Why though? Why take it? You couldn't have known that this would happen."

No. Having a creepy collector walk in when I had finally gathered up the nerve to kiss Rift, even on the cheek, I had not expected in any way. I had only been curious. "No. I wanted to learn more about it, and the only way to do that was to get it out of lockup."

I zipped my jacket and headed for the door, then stopped when I realized Rift wasn't following me. "What?"

"Where are you going?"

This time I unleashed the smirk in full force. Rift's feathery hair shifted back from his face as he raised his head. "Every item logged into evidence has a tracking device implanted, invisible to the naked eye. I'm going to track down the Barkeep. Would you like to help?"

Chapter Seventeen

Tracking down The Barkeep was almost pathetically easy. This time we did everything by the book. Cara and Elliott accompanied us, along with a few other officers just in case we needed backup. Rift and I led the way into the building, magic on our hands, and seeing The Barkeep's face when he'd discovered that I was lying to him about losing my magic was a joy to behold. Rift and I watched as he was led away in cuffs; a giant grin practically split my face in half.

Once all the paperwork was done, Rift and I went back to our apartment. I didn't know where Cara and Elliott had gone, and I honestly didn't care. I led Rift to the roof, staring up at the stars as we lie on our backs. I had brought a blanket to lay on, but with hard gravel, it didn't make much of a difference. Almost lazily I called to my magic, watching it swirl around my fingertips. Rift did the same. This time, there were no horses, but I had a better idea.

"Remember when you asked me what I was going to do when I got my magic back? And I didn't have an answer for you?"

Rift turned his head, a thick lock of hair falling into his face as he studied me. I was leaning up on one elbow but he was still on his back, looking up at me. He cocked one eyebrow warily. "Yes?"

"I figured it out." I concentrated for a moment, gathering magic into a small ball in my hand, then tossed it upward. The purple shattered, showering magic like a firework. The powder left behind hung in the shape of Rift's face, and I flushed. I'd never made a Magic Work like that before, only read about them; I hadn't known that it would put the face of the person I was thinking about out there for the entire world to see. Or if not the world, then at the very least most of the city. Rift sat up slowly, periwinkle magic gathering in his palm, then shot it skyward just as I had. My face appeared, outlined in blue and with much more detail than my portrait had had of him. I punched his arm lightly.

"What was that for?" he asked indignantly, rubbing the sore spot.

"Even your flipping magical fireworks are better than mine, and it was *my idea!* Can you *please* just cut me some slack already?"

He leaned forward, lips hovering near mine. "Are you sure you want me to?" I closed the distance between us, savoring the softness of his lips and the cool bite of the gum that we had both been chewing. I couldn't think of a more romantic setting, sitting on a city rooftop looking at the stars with magical fireworks shouting to the world how we felt about each other, and after awhile, I wasn't thinking at all.

Epilogue

Rift went back to his regular job, and I went back to mine. He left the city, but we sent each other both text and magical messages every day. I was finally settling back in at work, but there were so many new things that I wanted to learn about with Rift that I felt there wasn't enough time in the day. He wanted to learn more about why he and I could call each other's magic at will (we had discovered that the connection went both ways), and I wanted to know why it pretty much kept us up all night if we shared magic but not if we took it from one another. We both wanted to know how we were able to swap magic so completely, and for how long; we were concerned that it could someday be permanent, which is why we were careful not to push things too far.

There was still so much that I had to learn from Rift, and he from me, and plenty of things that we could learn from each other. Things had never been better. I could only hope they stayed that way.

THE END

About the Author

Julie Kramer is a USA Today bestselling author from a small town in Ohio, USA. When not attending college classes, she enjoys spending time with her family and her silly Husky, when she's not writing Young Adult fantasy novels.

Also by Julie Kramer

The Science of Dragons
The Journey of Dragons

Aerie of the Gryphons

Kings and Queens of War

Crystal Dark

Of Curses and Scandals

CPSIA information can be obtained
at www.ICGtesting.com
Printed in the USA
LVHW040751220620
658672LV00005B/1238